NATALIE MICHAELS

THE
WHITE
DAHLIA

VINCI
BOOKS

By Natalie Michaels

Steve Campbell Psychological Suspense Thrillers

The Last Girl

The Bone Forest

The White Dahlia

For D…
Appreciate your loved ones before they're gone

Vinci Books

vinci-books.com

Published by Vinci Books Ltd in 2025

1

A CIP catalogue record for this book is available from the British Library.
Paperback ISBN: 9781036707828

Chapter One

THE SURGEON

The Surgeon reached for the sponge in the bucket, squeezed as much water out of it, and wiped her thigh clean. He dropped the sponge in the bucket, squeezed water out of it, and wiped down her shin and ankle. He wiped over a dark mark, smudging it over the top of her foot. The lines between his eyes creased. He continued rubbing until the mark disappeared. He rinsed the sponge, squeezed the water out, and wiped over that same spot until he was content nothing spoiled her porcelain flesh.

He soaked the sponge, squeezed it dry, and wiped. After he finished cleaning every part of her, he emptied the bucket and added fresh water for another round of cleaning.

When he was satisfied she was clean, her skin snow white, the Surgeon reached for the scalpel and slashed the corners of her mouth until her smile reached her ears.

Her smile pleased him.

Then, for the finishing touches, he cut chunks of flesh

from her thighs and breasts, placing them in a sterile tray for later.

He picked up the delicate flower and placed it carefully behind her ear, ensuring it stayed there.

The Surgeon stared at her in wonder; the way her hair framed her face, how her unseeing blue eyes met his, and at the shell her soul once inhabited. *Her*.

He smiled, appreciating his masterpiece, something he'd never replicate.

She was one of a kind.

A doll to admire.

His muse.

His Dahlia.

His.

Chapter Two

Detective Steve Campbell

"Wait!" Alice yelled from the kitchen. "Your lunch," she said, running up to me with her hand raised, holding a brown bag.

I groaned inwardly. I still had a few pounds to lose, and Alice was adamant she would help me by making lunch daily instead of wasting money and buying delicious takeout burgers, pizzas, pastas, and anything with grease that clogged my arteries.

"Thanks, honey," I said, cupping her face and kissing her. She wrapped her arms around my waist, melting against my body, and dropped the lunch.

"Oh dear," she said, ending our kiss. "Your lunch."

"It's okay," I said, letting her go and crouching to pick it up. "What's in here?" I shook the heavy bag.

"An egg salad, and a sandwich with roast chicken and mayo on health bread." She smiled. "I know you get hungry, so I thought I'd make you two meals."

I beamed at her. She looked after me in all ways. "Thank you," I said, kissing her forehead. "I'll see you tonight."

"Will you be working late?" she asked with sadness in her tone.

"I doubt it. It's been two weeks since our last big case and things have settled down. From today, we're looking into that cold case." Yesterday we had finished reviewing all those recordings and it relieved me we could focus on something else.

Her smile returned, reaching her honey-colored eyes. "Dinner is at six."

"I'll be here," I said, grabbing my keys.

The drive to the police station in Ketchum was quiet for a Monday morning. There were moms pushing prams toward the park, joggers running their circuit, and dogs on leads with owners smiling happily.

I parked in my allocated spot in the basement and headed for my office. There weren't many detectives at Ketchum Police Station, therefore I was the only one with an office, apart from the captain, while the rest shared the open plan space next door.

Officer Graham entered my office with two coffees the moment I sat down. "Detective," he said in greeting. "Ready for the cold case?"

As much as I wanted to complain that I'd just arrived and needed a few minutes to settle in, I didn't want to kill his enthusiasm to solve cases. I smiled in response and placed my lunch on the 'In tray' beside my desk phone. "Absolutely," I said, opening my desk drawer.

"Here," Officer Graham said, handing me a folder and placing my coffee on the table.

The lines between my eyes deepened. "Is that it?" I asked, taking it from him.

"Yes, she's a Jane Doe, thought to be a runaway or a prostitute."

I opened the folder to a one-page statement and a detailed two-page autopsy report. The one-page statement provided bland facts about how they discovered her body and by whom. There were no follow-up interviews, no witness interviews, or pictures from all angles. There were four pictures; one from afar, the rest were closeups of her body parts. The way they had positioned our Jane Doe's body reminded me of something, but I couldn't quite place it.

"And this is from Dr. Brink." He handed me the results from the black cloth caught in a tree, and blood drops found on rocks. We had discovered the evidence together when investigating the murders at Sawtooth Forest near Bald Mountain.

"Thanks." I read the one-page statement written by a police officer who worked the Jane Doe case. "Have you called this police officer?"

"He retired the same year and died last year."

I glanced up at him, arching eyebrows. "Did anyone else work the case?"

He shook his head. "I called the previous coroner, Doc Lesley, who vaguely remembers the case. He said nobody claimed her body, nobody recognized her, and there was no evidence to process."

"So basically, he did nothing about her murder?"

"Yes."

"Were you here in 1997?" It was only five years ago, and Officer Graham had joined the force at least ten years earlier.

"I was, but I don't remember the case." He shrugged. "I've spoken to the captain about this case, and he is fuming because that officer didn't inform him about it at all. I don't think anybody knew about it except Doc Lesley."

That piqued my interest. "Do you think the police officer buried it on purpose?"

"Yes. It's the only logical explanation."

"This police station seems to have a reputation for removing evidence or hiding homicides." I was referring to the second case I had worked on since moving to Ketchum from Las Vegas, where the serial killer had paid off a police officer to move evidence involving his parent's death.

Officer Graham shifted uncomfortably, avoiding eye contact. "I'm waiting for the evidence to be sent to us so we can do a thorough investigation."

"Thanks," I said, standing, "but I don't feel like waiting. Let's fetch it now."

Officer Graham stood straighter and nodded, exiting my office after me.

Chapter Three

THE EVIDENCE

Detective Steve Campbell

I followed Officer Graham downstairs to the evidence storeroom. There was a pen and book tied to the desk where we had to sign in, along with the evidence we wanted. We were yet to upgrade our system, but for now everything was still old-school.

Officer Graham fished for the key as I was about to write in the book when Daphne, a junior officer, opened the gate from the other side.

"Is this what you're looking for?" she said, handing me the box.

I glanced at the label on the front, and it matched the case number in the file. "Yes, thanks Daphne."

"Pleasure Detective. There isn't much in there, but I'm sure you boys will solve it," she said. Her smile reaching her gray/green-colored eyes.

"We'll do the best we can," I said, tucking the box under

my arm. I was about to leave when I remembered. "Do we still have to fill in the book?"

"I'll do it for you," Daphne said, picking up the pen.

"Thanks," I said, noticing the ring on her finger. "Did you get engaged?"

Her smile reached her bright eyes. "Last night," she said, wiggling her fingers.

"Congratulations," Officer Graham said. "That was fast. Didn't you two only start dating a short while ago?"

"Yes," Daphne said, looking at me. "When you know you know, you know." She raised a shoulder.

"You aren't pregnant, are you?" Officer Graham asked. I shot him an annoyed look, but he was staring at Daphne.

"No," she grumbled, turning her back on him.

"Congrats, Daphne," I said, motioning for Officer Graham to leave. "Let us know when it is."

"Will do," she said, still busy with the book.

"What was that about?" I asked when we were out of earshot.

"Nothing," Officer Graham said in a huff.

"It didn't sound like nothing," I said, traversing up the stairs.

"The guy is a biker, Detective." He returned the annoyed look I'd given him earlier.

"Yeah, so?"

"Bikers are generally bad news. I'd hate for something bad to happen to her. She's too nice to marry someone like that."

I agreed with Officer Graham. Daphne was a lovely individual. She seemed gentle and highly sensitive, but we couldn't interfere in someone else's life. "Do you know the guy?"

"No, but—"

"But nothing, officer. It's Daphne's life and you aren't her ex-boyfriend or family. Until you have something concrete against this guy, leave it alone." I warned.

Officer Graham grumbled something I couldn't hear and walked off. I decided to leave it for now. We had a cold case to investigate.

I placed the box on our largest meeting room table and flicked off the lid. I stared at the contents. Inside was the victim's handbag that was found a short distance away from her body.

"Is that it?" Officer Graham asked, entering with the two coffees he had brought earlier. "I heated them." He handed me one. It relieved me his mood had improved. We had work to do.

"Yeah, this is it," I said. "Thanks for the coffee." I placed it beside the box. With a gloved hand, I opened the handbag and placed the contents out on the table; dark red lipstick, a business card for surgical devices, cash, loose tissues, and a fake flower clip. "Did they test these?"

Officer Graham placed the autopsy report and the one-page statement beside the purse. "No, there's nothing. They were just boxed and shelved."

"Call James and ask if he has time to process them now."

Officer Graham left the office to make the call. I picked up the warm coffee and sipped, wincing at the bitter taste. A shudder ran through me. I placed the stale coffee carefully inside the trashcan. I packed the items back inside the purse and placed them in the box, closing the lid. Removing the disposable gloves, I threw them in the trashcan and sat down.

The police officer who had investigated this case did a poor job. He failed to place each item inside individual bags to preserve any traces of DNA that may have still been on there. I doubted there would be anything for them to test after five years, but I still wanted it done.

"He's in the building and will be here shortly," Officer Graham said, entering the meeting room and sitting across from me.

It had been two weeks since I watched the video of a man resembling Officer Graham enter the evidence store-room and remove evidence. I couldn't see his face, but I recognized his strange gait; like he had an injured leg and limped. I still needed to address this with him, but I first wanted to see how things went and if Officer Graham had other extra-curricular activities I needed to know about. Like that old saying, keep your enemies close.

"Morning," James McIntosh said, wearing the widest smile.

"Someone is having a good morning," I said, feeling some relief from my thoughts and matched his smile.

"Well," he said with a flick of his wrist. "Hubby has arranged a getaway weekend for us, and I simply can't wait."

"Where are you going?" Officer Graham asked, twisting in his chair to look up at him.

"Like I'm sharing that. The last thing I need now is for you and the missus interrupting our fun," he said with a wink. "I'll send you the details when I get to my computer."

"Thanks," Officer Graham said, and visibly relaxed. Sometimes one didn't know where James was going with his 'jokes'.

"I'm amazed Dr. Brink gave you time off," I said, leaning forward and placing my elbows on the table.

"I have so much leave due, and she didn't want me losing

any of it. Besides, you know what it's like. They don't like paying us for leave we don't use," he said, shrugging. "I have the Friday and the Monday off. I think taking long weekends away often is better than having a long holiday only once a year."

"I agree," I said. "Which reminds me, I need to do something for Alice's birthday." I made a reminder in my notebook. There was that new Italian restaurant I'd been meaning to take her to, and a weekend away would be most welcome. I needed it now more than ever, especially after the last case.

"Yeah, don't forget," James said. "She'll enjoy it. And we all need to rest," he turned toward Officer Graham and elbowed him, "even you."

"I'm taking some leave in two months' time," Officer Graham said, grinning. "And I can't wait to soak up the beach sun."

James stepped closer to the table. "Anyway, what do you have for me?" he said, leaning on the table.

I opened the lid. "A purse and its contents."

"It looks vintage," James said, pulling the box closer. He reached for a pair of disposable gloves from his pocket and slipped them on. He picked up the purse, opened it, and peeked inside. "It should be quick."

"Thanks, James," I said. "Were you here in 1997?"

"Yes," he said, frowning. "Is that how old the case is?" He pointed at the box and returned the purse.

"Yes," I said. "And the investigating officer seemed to have closed the case before bothering to do any actual police work."

"Who was the officer?"

I read the one-page statement. "Officer Eugene Aldridge."

James arched eyebrows. "No surprise there. He was the most useless, lazy officer I'd ever worked with."

"How so?" I asked.

"Well, for one, he was always late, had sloppy evidence cataloguing, and never returned phone calls. I was glad he retired long before his time."

"I'm amazed Captain didn't fire him."

"He was conveniently married to Captain's aunt, so I can only assume he turned a blind eye towards the guy," James said, picking up the box.

It explained why Captain never knew about this case or why he didn't fire Eugene. "Thanks, James, it makes sense. Do you know if we can view old employee files?"

James chuckled. "Check with Captain." He raised a shoulder. "But I doubt you'll get anything."

I sighed audibly. He was probably right. It wasn't often we could view other officers' personal files, but this was an exception. This officer did nothing about this homicide case. How many times had this happened?

Captain's ears had to have been burning because he came in behind James. "Men," he said in his deep baritone. We knew he was nearby even when he whispered. "I hear you've taken on that Jane Doe case."

"Yes, sir," I said, standing. "Were you aware of this case Officer Eugene Aldridge had worked on?"

"No, I knew nothing about it, or I would've instructed him to do a better job. I'm sure you're aware he was married to my aunt." I nodded. "They divorced before I told him to retire in 1997 and then he disappeared," he continued. "I heard he had passed away last year from brain cancer."

"I don't suppose I can look at his employee file?"

"Why do you want that?" His brows squashed together,

making them look like a hairy caterpillar. Captain Emory Payne was a one-of-a-kind man; even his name was unusual. At first glance, he reminded me of a soft teddy bear with bushy eyebrows and wild curly hair, but he was the scariest Captain I'd ever worked with. Nobody took a chance with him, yet Eugene did.

"I would like to see if this was the only case he mishandled or if he did it regularly."

"You don't have to see his employee file because he mishandled everything he touched," Captain said. "Eventually, I gave him cases involving theft or break-ins. That's why I'm shocked to find out he worked a homicide case." Red blotches formed on Captain's neck and cheeks, so I thought it best to leave it for now, but I still wanted to see Eugene's file for any alleged allegations against him.

"Who were the officers who worked with him around that time?"

Captain shook his head, deep in thought. "Nobody wanted to, but he did work with Officer Beckett on one case."

"Thank you, sir," I said. I had only met Officer Beckett once. He was retiring soon and had a desk job doing odds and ends or wherever we needed him.

Chapter Four

OLD PARTNERS

Detective Steve Campbell

Officer Beckett wasn't at his desk. Then, as I walked back to my office, someone deep in thought headed my way. The tall man had the longest legs I'd ever seen before, and his feet seemed to float with each step.

"Officer Beckett," I said, waving at him.

"Detective?" he said with confusion stamped all over his face. "Nobody comes down here."

I smiled. He was the only one here in the chilly bowels of the Records Department. "I'm working a cold case and the officer who handled it didn't do a great job. I heard you had partnered with him once or twice—"

"Eugene Aldridge?" His face contorted with bitterness and rage.

I smiled. "Yes, him."

Officer Beckett rolled his eyes. "He was a waste of space and annoying. I don't know how he even got a job here."

"Do you think he was lazy, or would he not do certain tasks on purpose?"

"He was lazy and conniving. I never trusted him." He rolled his shoulders. "He had dark beady eyes you just knew not to trust. But to answer your question, he knew what he was not doing, so it wouldn't surprise me if he did it on purpose. And if he got money out of it, even better."

"Did you hear him talk about a homicide case in nineteen-ninety-seven?"

"No." He shook his head. "He wasn't supposed to work homicide."

"Yeah, that's what we're finding strange."

"I'd look into that if I were you," Officer Beckett said.

"Thanks, we will," I said, shaking his hand. At least now I had a clearer idea about who Eugene Aldridge was and that perhaps I shouldn't trust anything he wrote in the case file.

Chapter Five

AUTOPSY REPORT

Detective Steve Campbell

Around lunchtime I sat in the meeting room again to read the autopsy report for our Jane Doe in detail. Officer Graham was doing his own research at his desk.

I opened the file;

Jane Doe
1.66cm tall
55kgs
Light blue eyes
Brown hair
Decaying teeth
Ligature marks on her ankles, wrists, and neck. With irregular laceration and superficial tissue loss on her right breast. Superficial laceration on right forearm, left upper arm, and lower left side of chest.
Body cut in half. Lower half removed by transecting the lumbar spine between second and third lumbar vertebrae, severing the intestines at...

I stopped reading. Jane Doe's case sounded exactly like an unsolved murder.

"The Black Dahlia," Officer Graham said from the doorjamb.

"What?" I sounded as confused as I felt.

"Our Jane Doe's murder is almost exactly like the Black Dahlia from fifty years ago."

"What date was she found?"

"The 15th of January 1947."

"Exactly fifty years ago." I pointed at the date we found our Jane Doe.

"It's almost as if—"

"They did it on purpose."

"Exactly." Officer Graham sat across from me, waving the paper he had in his hand. "We need to view the scene where Officer Aldridge found her body and judging from the pictures and the information we have on The Black Dahlia, I suspect we'll see more similarities."

I rubbed my face. "How did Eugene not see this?"

"Maybe he did," Officer Graham said.

I studied the gruesome photos; they had cut Jane Doe's body in half above her pelvic bones, her legs spread apart, and the top half of her body a short distance away with her arms raised above her head.

"I don't suppose you have a picture of The Black Dahlia's crime scene?"

"Here," he said, handing me the printout. "And here is her autopsy report."

I read the information, then placed both autopsy reports side by side.

"They're almost identical," Officer Graham said. "It's eerie."

"You can say that again." The description of Jane Doe's

body in the autopsy report was almost word for word identical to The Black Dahlia's autopsy. The same type of lacerations, where they had cut her body in half, how they had ruined her face when the killer extended the corners of her mouth to her ears. And our Jane Doe had bruising on her head, most likely from repeated blows. In both autopsy reports, the coroner indicated signs of sodomy but negative for sperm.

"I've checked our system and can't see what happened to her body. So, I asked Dr. Brink to see if her body isn't still there, and if she can perform a second autopsy."

"Good thinking, maybe she can find something this time around," I said, leaning back in the chair. "The similarities are too close to ignore, so I suggest we study The Black Dahlia case to see if we can get leads in our case."

Officer Graham nodded as he made notes. "I'll contact the FBI to get copies of their files."

"Thanks," I said, standing. "Let's take a drive to the scene?"

Officer Graham stared at his notes with concern.

"What's wrong?"

"Do you think the FBI will want our case?"

"Doubtful," I said, feeling concerned. "Maybe they have enough on their plate." I hoped.

Chapter Six

CRIME SCENE

Detective Steve Campbell

Officer Graham drove the ten minutes to the area where a mother with her child discovered Jane Doe in 1997. Five years ago, the area was an open field, now there were houses.

Officer Graham parked on the sidewalk so that he didn't obstruct traffic. We exited the vehicle and headed toward the area that looked like the photographs.

"This could be the spot," I said, raising my hand holding the photograph. I positioned the photograph in such a way that it aligned with the sidewalk perfectly. There were similar dents in the cement, and a pole that now held a working light. "And there they found her handbag."

"They positioned her body here," Officer Graham said, pointing at an area. In the photo, the land was uneven and barren; now grass grew beautifully for the family who owned the piece of land. "They removed her intestines and placed them under her buttocks here." He pointed at the area.

"Like The Black Dahlia," I said, holding the photo that showed our Jane Doe's body parts. Then I raised the photo of The Black Dahlia.

"Do you think he's a copycat killer?" Officer Graham asked.

"I honestly don't know what to think." I stepped forward and crouched. "The lower half of her body had to have been here if I look at the photo. While the top part there," I said, pointing at the various areas. I stood and surveyed the area. "It's a quiet neighborhood."

Officer Graham nodded and mumbled, "Yeah".

"Five years ago, there were no houses here," I continued. "Across the road is the same building with various businesses, but none would've been open that time of the morning. And down there," I pointed to our far left, "was The Lodge." I closed the folder with a picture showing the area five years ago and walked the short distance to The Lodge, that was open around the time her body was spotted.

"Do you think they saw her body?" Officer Graham asked.

"That's what I'm hoping to find out."

"I've been here twice," Officer Graham said, running to catch up to me. "A lunch with the wife, and dinner with friends."

"Do you know anyone who works there?"

"My uncle used to work there when the old man still ran the place." He shrugged. "Doubt he'll know anyone now."

I opened the door and entered. The smell of fries, bacon, and stale alcohol wafted in the air. The restaurant on my right was open for business. In front was the reception area, a corridor on the left, and a set of elevators leading to the rooms.

A tall, dark man approached, smiling. "Welcome to The Lodge. How may I help you today?"

His name tag read Phillip. Gray hair peppered the sides of his dark hair and the goatee he sported. He wore a fancy suit and smelled like Old Spice.

"I'm Detective Campbell and this is Officer Graham. Is there anyone we can speak with who worked here five years ago?"

Phillip frowned but continued, smiling politely. "I worked here five years ago, but you'll probably want to speak with the owner." He spun on his heel and headed down the corridor. "Follow me."

"Do you remember any murders that took place around here in 1997?" I asked, almost jogging to keep up with Phillip.

Phillip was quiet and slowed his steps. "There was something that happened early in the year, but I don't recall the details, and it wasn't in the newspaper; which I found strange."

"Can you tell me what you remember?"

"Nothing, really," Phillip said, stopping outside an office. "There was commotion early January, and those that went outside to look had said it was a dead woman. I didn't go because I faint at the sight of blood," he raised a shoulder, "and that's the last I heard of it."

"I don't suppose you remember who all went outside to look?" I asked, reaching for the pen in the folder.

"He did," Phillip thumbed at the door behind him, "Julian Holmes, Grace Clark, Brian Smith, Jozef Martinez, Stephen Evens, and Scott Walker."

I arched both eyebrows. "That's quite a memory."

Phillip didn't remember details but remembered all those who looked.

"I don't know the details of what the woman looked like, but I have a sharp memory of everything else."

I wished I had his memory. "Do they still work here?" I asked.

Phillip nodded and knocked on the door.

"What?" a man barked from the other side of the door.

Phillip rolled his eyes. "Brace yourself," he whispered and entered.

"You should be out front," the man said from behind his desk. He didn't bother looking up, but he did when I spoke.

"I'm Detective Campbell and this is Officer Graham," I said, raising my I.D. "We would like to speak with you about a woman murdered five years ago."

The man behind the desk flinched, then visibly relaxed. "Um, yeah, sure, sit over there, and make yourself comfortable," he said nervously, pointing at the two seats in front of his desk. "Bring our guests some coffee."

"Yes, sir," Phillip said, closing the door behind him.

"What do you need?" The nameplate on his desk read 'Gen. Manager Daniel Hanson'.

I made notes of his name. "Five years ago a woman was murdered," I started, "her body cut in half."

Daniel shifted uncomfortably in his chair. He scratched the side of his head, lifting brown hair, then scratched the sides of his mustache. When I thought he was done fidgeting, he pulled the sleeves of his neatly pressed navy suit. "I vaguely remember something like that." He glanced up and to his left, then stared at me without blinking. He was lying.

"She had brown hair, light blue eyes, and her smile surgically enlarged against her will."

Daniel cleared his throat. "Oh yes, yes, I remember now," he said, pulling himself closer to the desk.

"What can you tell us about that day?"

"Not much," Daniel said, staring at the wall to my side. "There was a commotion outside. Some of us went and looked and we found a woman in two pieces, and someone had given her the scariest smile." He visibly shuddered. "It was horrible. Not a drop of blood anywhere," he said, finally looking me in the eye.

"Did you know the woman?"

"I'd seen her around." He picked up a pen and flicked the top a few times.

"Did you know her name?"

Sweat peppered his forehead. "Like I said, I'd seen her around but didn't really know her."

"And the policeman—"

"What about him?"

"Did he say anything to those at the crime scene? Ask for statements? That kind of thing?"

Daniel shrugged. "I don't remember. I don't think so. He was by himself until the meat wagon came along and took her body away. Then everyone left."

"Can we speak with those who came to look? Phillip gave us a list of those he remembered."

Daniel glanced at the door as it opened, and Phillip entered holding a tray with coffee.

"I'm glad he could be helpful," Daniel said, staring deadpan at Phillip.

"Thanks," I said, taking the mug from the tray.

Once everyone had their coffee, Phillip left, and Daniel continued. "Here is the list," he said, handing me a piece of paper with names and telephone numbers. I checked it against the list Phillip had given me, and they matched except one.

"Can I have your phone number?"

"Why?" Daniel said. "You're talking to me now."

"Just in case we have follow-up questions." I handed back the piece of paper. "Thanks," I said, taking it back from him after he added his details, and slipping it inside the folder. "Do you know of anyone who may know the woman's name or was with her the days leading up to her death?"

Daniel leaned into his chair back and steepled his fingers. "Charlie Roberts."

"Who is he?"

"He owns a restaurant named *'Charlie's'*. He knew the girl very well."

"Thanks," I said, standing. I placed a business card on his table. "Please call me if you remember anything about that day."

"Sure," Daniel said, taking the card and placing it in the desk top drawer.

I finished my coffee and placed it on the tray on the table near the door. Officer Graham did the same. Before we left his office, I noted a stunning black-and-white photograph of a woman. Then, as Officer Graham closed the door, Daniel was on the phone with someone.

"Let's see what Charlie has to say," I said.

Chapter Seven

CHARLIE'S

Detective Steve Campbell

Since moving to Ketchum I hadn't had much time for sightseeing since I was too busy working cases, but I recalled seeing Charlie's when driving past.

'Charlie's' occupied an entire block on the main road in Ketchum; one side it had a sports bar for the young and restless, while the other side families could come and enjoy a meal any time of the day. It was well past lunchtime, and it was full.

"Do you have a reservation?" A woman with thick, black, drawn on eyebrows said. I noticed nothing but her eyebrows.

I held up my I.D. "We'd like to speak with Charlie Roberts."

"Yes, sure," she said, picking up the receiver and pressed numbers. "Hey Charlie, there's a couple of cops here to see you," she said, glancing at us. "Yeah, yeah, okay." She nodded and ended the call. "He's expecting you." She pointed down the corridor which servers used. "There's a sign. Just go up the stairs. His is the only office there."

Someone entered the restaurant behind us, and the woman helped them, forcing us to one side.

"Well, let's go see the man," Officer Graham said, heading up the stairs first.

The smell from the kitchen as a server exited made my stomach grumble. I'd already eaten, yet I could easily eat again. I traversed up the stairs begrudgingly.

Officer Graham stopped, and I almost walked into him. I came around his side and found Charlie Roberts standing with his arms folded over his chest, his belly hanging low and over his belt, and his dark brown, almost black, eyes glaring daggers at us. "I don't have all day, so ask your questions so I can get back to work."

"Hi, I'm Detective Steve Campbell," I said in my friendliest voice, and proffered a hand.

"Officer Graham," Officer Graham said, also proffering a hand.

Charlie stared at our hands like there was dirt on them, and the muscles along his jaw ticked.

"I take it Daniel Hanson has already spoken with you regarding this cold case we're working?" I lowered my hand.

"Yes," Charlie said, fisting his right hand.

"What was her name?" I asked.

"Ella Turner. She was twenty-three, and a wonderful girl." Charlie Roberts was in his late forties. He was bald on top with salt and pepper colored hair on the sides. Based on the indent his wedding ring had left on his naked finger, he'd been married a long time. I wondered why he'd taken it off.

"What kind of relationship did you have with her?" I

wrote her name in my notebook, relieved we had something to work with.

"I saw her once or twice a week," he said deadpan. "Took her for dinner, maybe some dancing. She was very naïve, so I helped her a lot about life and offered suggestions."

"Were you married at the time?" The killer had cut Ella's body in two and sliced her face open. This was personal, a crime of passion; perhaps it was either him or his wife.

"Yes, and before you run off accusing me or my wife of harming that poor girl, she knew about it, and she knows about my current girlfriend. We are an open-minded couple who love to explore and share. You're welcome to ask her yourself."

I stared at him with a mouth full of teeth when he shared information about his open marriage and was relieved when Officer Graham asked the next question.

"Was Ella involved with anyone else, and where were you her last night?"

"It was one of the rare occasions I was with my wife. Ella and I had a loose relationship, if I could call it that. I had my life, and she had hers. I don't know who else she was seeing, but there were others."

"Did you ever pay her?" I asked. Someone had suggested our Jane Doe, Ella Turner, may have been a call girl or prostitute.

Charlie's lip twitched. "I paid nothing, but," he held up a hand, "I bought her gifts, sometimes food. That kind of thing."

"Do you have an address where she stayed?"

"It was an apartment in Oak Street, The Highrise, I think. Apartment 109."

"One last question. Do you know of anyone who wanted to hurt her?"

"No," he said sadly, glancing away, "she was a lovely girl. When Daniel called me that day telling me someone murdered Ella, it left me devastated. She never hurt anyone. I don't know who could've done such a horrific thing. It was barbaric."

It seemed we needed to speak with Daniel again; he knew who she was, yet he sent us to Charlie. I glanced at Officer Graham knowingly, who nodded in response.

"Do you remember if any police asked follow-up questions?" I asked.

"There was only one cop who spoke with everyone at the scene. He took our names and numbers, but I never heard from anyone. I'm unsure if any of the others were contacted."

I didn't see a list with their information on in the file. Officer Aldridge must've destroyed it.

"Thank you for your time," I said. "Here's my card if you think of anything else." I handed him my card.

"Sure," Charlie said, looking at it, then turning it over before pocketing it.

As we exited the restaurant, a man wearing a vintage white fedora hat with a black band glanced up from his coffee and stared at us. I couldn't see his face, but I wouldn't forget those piercing eyes.

Once outside, the late afternoon sun warmed my face and I was ready to leave, but I couldn't get that man's questionable glare out of mind. I turned around and went back inside. Officer Graham mumbled something, but I ignored him. I pushed past a crowd who had entered when we exited and once I was through the crowd and near his table, only to find it empty.

"Is there an exit somewhere else?" I asked the front lady, interrupting the old man, who was asking about his reservation.

"Um, yes," she stammered, "out back." She thumbed behind her.

I hurried between the tables and went around the other side to the emergency exit. I pushed the doors open as a car sped away. Officer Graham came in behind me, panting.

"What was that?" he asked.

"I don't know, but we need to know who that was."

"I don't know what to tell you. His reservation was under A. Nadmirer." The hostess's hands shook as she paged through the Bookings book.

"Has he been in here before?" I asked. My voice raised.

"No, sir, it was the first time I'd seen him." She chewed on her bottom lip. "Maybe the other hostess knows him." She tapped on the security screen, but he'd concealed his face the entire time he was drinking his coffee.

"Thanks," I said, needing to calm down and not scare the help. "I appreciate your assistance."

"What does that mean?" Officer Graham asked as we exited the restaurant.

"Only that he's An Admirer of the case."

"A Nadmirer, An Admirer. Okay, I get it." Officer Graham closed his car door. "Spooky, considering we've only just started investigating."

"Or word got around quickly thanks to Daniel and he's the killer and wants to know how far we've gotten."

Chapter Eight

ELLA TURNER

Detective Steve Campbell

Now that we had more information on the victim, along with her name, we headed back to the station to regroup and do a little digging before heading to the apartment block.

Officer Graham was looking into the names given to us by Phillip and Daniel, and I'd investigate the victim.

I typed in Ella Turner's name into the system and there were two people sharing that name, but only one matching her description and had lived here. To say that I was a little shocked to see her in the system was an understatement, but at the same time, it relieved me because we had more information on her, along with some of her background.

Ella Turner had the prettiest mugshot I'd ever seen. Her curly brown hair framed her delicate features beautifully, and if it wasn't for the number and her name at the bottom of the picture, anyone would've thought it was a professional black-and-white photoshoot.

In 1993, Colorado police arrested Ella Turner for underage drinking. She was eighteen, and the man she was with was ten years older.

Her father, Duncan Turner, arrested for a DUI in 1995 and in 1997 a day after her death. Had someone found out and told him, or was it purely coincidental?

Ella and Duncan shared the same addresses in Colorado until she turned twenty-one, then she moved here. According to her D.M.V. records, she stayed at 109 The Highrise. At least Charlie was telling the truth.

"Ella is in the system," I said, standing near Officer Graham's desk.

"Then how come we couldn't identify her?"

"I'd love to know," I said, feeling annoyed that Officer Aldridge had buried this case. "Doc Lesley would've picked this up."

"I don't know what to say, Detective. Doc Lesley would never help Officer Aldridge, and when I spoke with him, he never mentioned anything about her fingerprints."

"Yeah," I said, deep in thought. Doc Lesley was old in 1997, and only retired this year, 2002; which made him very old. I had nothing against old people who still worked, but after a certain age they were forgetful. "Anyway, we're on the case now and will do everything to solve it. Are you ready?" I asked.

"Yeah, sure, let me just finish this quickly." He made notes in his folder and stood. "I only looked into two of the names and so far, they're fine." He shrugged. "They have no records and have always worked at The Lodge."

"We can continue tomorrow," I said, shaking my car keys. "I want to go over to the apartment to find out if anyone knew our victim."

Chapter Nine

109 THE HIGHRISE

Detective Steve Campbell

Officer Graham knocked on the door and we waited. Someone inside the apartment yelled they were on their way. I didn't know what to expect since Ella Turner had lived here five years ago. Whether this person knew Ella, we were yet to find out.

Officer Graham raised his hand to knock again when the door opened. "Can I help you?" A young woman asked, pushing her thin silver framed glasses up her nose.

"I'm Detective Campbell and this is Officer Graham," I said, raising my I.D. for her to see.

"What's this about?" she asked, squinting.

"How long have you lived here?" I asked.

"About ten years," she said, opening the door wider to get a better view of our I.D.'s.

Officer Graham pocketed his I.D. "Did you have any roommates?"

"I've had a few. Why?"

"Was she one of your roommates?" I said, holding a picture up of Ella.

"Yeah, but she disappeared."

"What's your name?" Officer Graham asked, pulling out his notebook.

"Jessica Wilkins." The lines between her eyes deepened. "Why are you asking these questions?"

"Would you mind if we came inside?"

"Yeah," she said, hesitating, "sure." She glanced nervously between us but obliged, opening the door wider. "I bought this place with the money my parents left me after they passed away and rented out the spare bedroom to help make ends meet." Jessica traversed farther inside her apartment, giving us space to enter.

I closed the door behind me. The cozy apartment had two large windows which brightened the open-plan lounge and kitchen area. There was a guest bathroom on my left, and down the hallway were the two rooms and another bathroom.

"The day Ella arrived here from Colorado," Jessica continued, "we became instant friends, and I asked her if she wanted to rent my other room. The roommate I had got married and moved out the week before."

"Were you friends before she moved here, or did you meet in Ketchum?"

"I met her at The Lounge when I was still a waitress there. She had a white dahlia flower in her ear, and she reminded me of an innocent girl. We started speaking, and we got along well. She seemed kind and a little scared, with nowhere to go. I couldn't leave her. She came home with me that night, and we shared the apartment for a couple of years and then one day she didn't come home."

I found it interesting that Ella's first stop after arriving in

Ketchum was at The Lounge; where Daniel worked, yet he said nothing. A plausible explanation was he hadn't seen her that day, or he just didn't know.

"Do you know what happened to Ella?" I asked.

"No," Jessica said, reaching for the coffeepot. "Coffee?" she asked.

"No thanks," Officer Graham said.

"I'm good," I said. "Why didn't you file a missing person's report?"

"I thought she left town with her boyfriend."

"Who was her boyfriend?"

"Uh, she actually had a few. Her job wasn't exactly paying well, if you know what I mean." Jessica's voice went up a notch.

"No, we don't know. How about you tell us everything you can remember?"

Jessica made herself a cup of coffee and sat at the island in her kitchen. We sat across from her.

"Ella stayed by me for about two years," Jessica said, then sipped from her mug. "She worked as an office assistant for a businessman, but she wasn't paid right and then the business closed suddenly. I don't know what happened, but she desperately needed another job so she waitressed for a bit. Then she stopped doing that, yet she always had money. At first, I couldn't understand it until I saw her with a man one night and a different man the next. When I confronted her about it, because I didn't want no trouble, she said they were her friends, and they gave her money." Jessica made air quotes when she said, *gave her money*.

"Can you remember the name of the businessman and her other friends?" I asked.

Jessica thought for a moment and shrugged. "The businessman had an office near the post office selling surgical equipment. For the life of me, I remember no names, but I remember faces and places. The two men I'd seen her with were at The Lounge and Charlies."

"I may know the businessman she's referring to," Officer Graham said, making notes in his book without glancing my way. "I've seen it a few times when I went to the post office."

"What happened to her?" Jessica said. "Is she in trouble?"

"We discovered Ella's body five years ago in that open field near The Lounge."

Jessica gasped, covering her mouth and stared wide eyed. Then she glanced at the stack of letters. "But why ask about her now if she died five years ago? Why didn't anyone come see me then?"

"There are lots of reasons we can't go into right now," I said, not wanting to divulge much. "Here's my card if you think of anything else." I stood and headed for the door.

"Thank you." Jessica followed us.

"Before we go," I said. "If you had seen her with these men and thought she left with one of them. Did you see these men again after the fact?"

Jessica paled. "Um," she stammered, glancing at something behind me.

I turned around and headed for the letters.

"No wait," she said, running to the letters before I could get to them, slamming her palm on top. "When she disappeared and nobody came looking for her, I cashed the checks her late mom's estate sent her monthly." She searched for the envelope and reluctantly handed it to me. "I know, I know, I shouldn't have, but," she raised both shoulders, "I needed the money."

I made a mental note that we needed to follow up on Ella's parents, especially her mother's estate.

"Is her stuff still here?"

"Yes, of course," Jessica said, heading toward the first bedroom. "I cashed her check, therefore I ensured her room remained as she left it for when she returned."

It looked as though Ella's room had frozen in time, waiting for us to collect evidence. I smiled at Officer Graham, who grinned back. This might be the break in our case. Without saying a word, Officer Graham excused himself to call James, our lab technician.

"Did Ella leave a note saying where she was going or who she was with that last evening?"

"No," Jessica said. "She came and went as she pleased. And I never checked her room after she left. The only thing I do here is vacuum, and ensure it remains tidy. I don't mind if you look around. Please excuse me, I need to phone my manager to let her know I'll be late for my shift."

I pulled on a pair of disposable gloves and opened the closet, pushing hangers with clothing to one side. There were three pairs of heels and a pair of sneakers on the floor. The top shelf held boxes filled with keepsake but no pictures or anything of value.

I headed for the pillow and picked it up, feeling everywhere, but there was nothing. Then I checked under the mattress; nothing. There was nothing of importance on top of the vanity table. I opened the vanity table drawers, but there was nothing of value until I checked the top part inside of the drawer; a section came loose, revealing a secret compartment.

I paged through the diary and at first glance it was her ramblings about her days, some poems, but I focused on the last entry in the diary; 14 January 1997;

Charlie wants to see me again, but I need to rest a bit. I'm exhausted. I love my men. All of them. They take care of me as I take care of them. We have an understanding. And it's our love that keeps us together… but sometimes I need time to myself. Sometimes I just need to be left alone. And right now I want nothing to do with any of them.

Kevin wants to see me soon, but I'll see how I feel. He's promised he'll leave his wife, but I doubt it. They've been through so much and separating isn't on the cards for them. Apparently, he has a surprise for me, and I can't wait; I hope it's something beautiful.

Then there's my Daniel. He's the only one I can count on.

No matter how I feel, I'm grateful I have them in my life.

I had a suspicion who the men were she was referring to, but the only one we hadn't met yet was Kevin.

"I think I know who Daniel and Charlie are," I said, holding up the diary for Jessica to see when she returned from making her phone call, "but who is Kevin?"

Chapter Ten

DINNER WITH FRIENDS

Detective Steve Campbell

I arrived home in time to smell the heavenly food, and hear the clanking of dishes. I entered the open plan space with a deep sigh of relief, but when my eyes drifted to the guest sitting at the table, tension formed between my shoulders.

"Hi," Olivia said, beaming.

"Hi Olivia, I didn't know you were joining us for dinner," I said, hanging my coat on the rack and placing my gun in the table drawer near the front door, locking it. "Welcome back. How are you doing?" I asked. I had a long day on the new case and wanted a quiet dinner with Alice, but we hadn't seen Olivia since John, known as Dark_Chambers, had hurt her two weeks ago.

"I'm okay," Olivia said, glancing at her fingers in her lap. When she looked up again, tears welled in her eyes. "I spent these two weeks in a facility that assists trauma survivors reach the next step in our lives so that we can move on safely and today is my first day home. Alice was adamant I join you for dinner. I hope that's okay?"

"That's perfect," I said. "The least we can do is feed you."

"Hi honey," Alice yelled from the kitchen. "I hope you don't mind?"

"Not at all," I called back, smiling, and sat at the head of the table with Olivia on my left. I enjoyed a long drink of my ice water, the refreshing liquid cooling my throat. "I'm glad you're okay. Are you ready for the next step?"

"I think so," Olivia said, fidgeting with her fingers. "It all happened so quickly, and the recovery ended almost abruptly. It will take time for me to adjust, but I'll be fine." She didn't sound convinced. What those men had done to all the women, including Olivia and Violet, would take many years of self-love, compassion, and kindness to work through. It was awful.

"Are you still going to work in Violet's shop?"

"Yes, she's expecting me tomorrow and said I was welcome to leave early if I wanted to. She's been very supportive."

"I spoke with Violet a couple of days ago and she's recovered, but I think you two ladies need to look after each other."

"We will."

Alice arrived with our plates, setting one in front of me and the other in front of Olivia.

"I can't help but think there was something we missed, you know," Olivia said, poking her fork at the sliced meat with mint jelly on top. "But it could just be my imagination."

"We went through everything again after we killed Erik and arrested John. We've reviewed all those awful recordings. But if you remember something that points us to another person, let me know, because John hasn't spoken and is awaiting trial."

"Maybe it's that," Olivia said, deep in thought. "Maybe it's because John's trial hasn't started yet. The entire event leaves me uncomfortable."

"Right," Alice said, placing her plate in front of her and sitting down. "Eat before it gets cold."

We ate dinner in a comfortable silence, and the entire time, my mind replayed Olivia's comment. I always wondered whether we had gotten all the culprits in that horrific case. We had watched those awful snuff films produced by the two men accused, yet I too had a sneaky suspicion there may be more evil-doers.

"Hon," Alice said, pulling me out of my thoughts. I glanced up and smiled. "Are you ready for dessert?"

"Always," I said, finishing my meal and handing her my empty plate.

The two women continued talking in the kitchen about the therapy Olivia still needed to do now that she was out of the hospital. I stood and switched on the player and turned down the volume, leaving it loud enough we could still hear the music. The women returned with bowls of ice cream and chocolate sauce.

"You have outdone yourself again," I said, kissing Alice on the cheek. "Dinner was delicious."

"Pleasure," Alice said, blushing. "I went to the market this afternoon and saw the newspaper where they mentioned a cold case has resurfaced."

My spine stiffened, and I lowered my spoon. "Oh, what did it say?" I knew none of us gave an interview with any reporter, therefore somebody was leaking the story.

"I saved it for you," she said, reaching for her bag on the table behind her and handing me the clipping.

I read the article, and the heading caught my attention; *'The White Dahlia murder thawed for another investigation.'* The article listed two officers had started looking into the cold case and if anyone had information leading to the arrest of the killer that they should contact the newspaper. Now all I had to do was wait for Captain Payne to call us in for the leak.

"Mind if I keep this?" I asked, folding the article in two.

"It's all yours."

Chapter Eleven

THE MOTEL

Detective Steve Campbell

"I hope this is the Motel," Officer Graham said grumpily. I'd never heard him complain so much as he did today.

"There aren't many more for us to check," I said, opening the office door for the Roadside Inn.

"Good morning fellows," a man behind the desk said, combing his fingers through his oily hair. He smiled, revealing perfect but stained teeth. "Room by the hour or day?" he said with a wink.

I raised my I.D. "We would like to ask you a few questions."

"Oh," he said, standing straight with his shoulders back. He closed the book in front of him and moved closer to the exit on his left.

"Were you working here five years ago?"

He nodded. "Yeees," he drawled.

"Do you remember this woman coming here with

anyone?" I asked. Officer Graham had the folder with him and raised the photo of Ella.

The man took the picture from Officer Graham. His dirty fingers leaving oily smudges on the back of the photo. Officer Graham glanced at me, scowling. I raised a shoulder. As much as I would love to tell the guy to wash his hands, I wanted to get out of here soonest.

"She looks familiar," he said, handing the photo back. "Every New Year, we host a party. Let me grab the album." The man disappeared into the room behind him, the beads dangling from the door jamb clanking against each other.

I glanced around the room; an air conditioner whirred overhead, silver paper attached to it dancing in the wind. A stand to my left held postcards featuring Ernest Hemingway, and behind me near the door was a stand filled with old books and magazines from the eighties.

"Yeah," the man said, returning, holding up two photos. "She was here for the Valentine's and New Year's parties in 1996."

I took the photos from him. "Excellent memory," I said.

"What can I tell ya? I'm good with faces."

At the Valentine's party, a youthful Ella was leaning against a man resembling a younger Charlie, who was completely out of it. His shirt had white chunks of something on it.

"Doesn't look like Charlie can handle his alcohol," Officer Graham said over my shoulder. As much as I liked Officer Graham, anyone standing behind me looking at the item in my hands left me on edge.

I nodded, handing him that photo and turned sideways to look at the Christmas party picture in peace. In this one, Ella was thinner, making her look ten years older than she was. Her left eye pulled to the side, a sign of intoxication.

"Jeezuz," Officer Graham said over my shoulder again.

I sighed and handed him the picture.

"I wonder who that is?" Officer Graham pointed at the man possessively holding Ella. She was sitting on his lap with her left arm around his shoulder.

"I'd also want to know who he is," I said, pointing at the man staring at Ella in the distance. Shadows danced on his face, painting his features sinisterly. "Do you know who these men are?" I asked the Office Clerk.

"I've kept everything from the day I started here," he said, heading into the back room and returning a moment later with two books. "1996 and 1997," he said, raising the heavy items. "She was a pretty girl," he said, licking the corner of his mouth. "She always had a flower in her hair." He paged through the books, forwards, backwards, then forward again. "Here we go." He turned the book around so that I could see the entry.

Chapter Twelve

LITTLE WHITE LIES

Detective Steve Campbell

We met James at The Highrise. "Sorry for only getting to this now," he said as he traversed up the stairs. "Yesterday was hectic."

"No problem," I said when we reached her floor. "We're here now. I hope there's something useful we could use."

Officer Graham knocked on the door.

Jessica opened without making us wait, and welcomed us in.

"Have you dusted the room or left your fingerprints anywhere?" James asked Jessica.

"No, sir," Jessica said. "I've only vacuumed every other week."

"And you removed nothing?" James said.

"No, sir, nothing."

"Did you attend these parties with Ella?" I asked, holding up the photos the Office Clerk at the Roadside Inn gave us.

"I went to the Christmas party with her." Jessica took the photo and stared.

"Does she look intoxicated to you?" I asked.

"Yeah, I remember what happened. It was so long ago I'd forgotten about that night." She shook her head. "That was the night she got into a fight with Kevin." She handed the photo back. "He was possessive of her. Hated that she had other boyfriends, but he did nothing about it. He only liked to complain, then sulk."

"Do you know where we can find him?"

"No, sorry," she said.

"Do you know who he is?" I pointed at the man in the background.

"No," she said, biting her bottom lip. "I don't know who he is."

We were yet to enquire whether the businessman who sold surgical equipment was still around, and we'd do that soon.

"Ma'am," James said, entering the living area. "Are you sure you dusted nothing in that room?" he said, arching an eyebrow.

"Uh," Jessica said, glancing at her hands. "Just a little. The place was such a mess I neatened it when she didn't return home."

James sighed frustratingly and shook his head. "There are no fingerprints, men. And I found nothing of importance to process."

"Why didn't you say you cleaned?" I asked, my voice raised.

Jessica paled. "I'm sorry, but I panicked. Her room was a mess, she had clothing everywhere, had overturned her trashcan, and papers littered the floor. Her room always looked like a bomb had hit it, but that evening even more so."

I pinched the bridge of my nose. "I don't suppose you kept the papers?"

"No," Jessica said. "I'm sorry if I ruined things, but that girl ruined my life first. If it wasn't for her, I would've been married." The moment she said the words, she covered her mouth with her hands.

My spine stiffened. "Jessica," I said. My tone was bitter. The moment we met Jessica and started asking questions, the more she lied. "We can do this here or at the station, but you need to tell us exactly what happened."

Jessica apologized for hiding things from us and said everything she had told us was the truth. She didn't know what had happened to Ella, or who may have hurt her. She also gave us items she kept, thinking it might come in handy one day.

We helped James pack his things along with the items Jessica had given us; a fake white dahlia flower clip Ella wore, a promise ring from Kevin, and another diary James had found hidden in the closet in a box. There were prints on all the items for processing.

"Did Captain get hold of you?" James asked as he closed his car door.

"About the newspaper article?" I asked.

Officer Graham raised both eyebrows. "What article?"

"Someone at the local newspaper has written a story on our victim, naming her the White Dahlia," I said.

"Like the Black Dahlia?" James said. "The cases are eerily similar."

"Yeah," I said, handing Officer Graham the article.

He whistled. "I wonder who the leak is?"

"It could be any of the witnesses we've spoken to," I said, folding the article and pocketing it again. "Let's get back to the office and sort this out with the captain."

Captain Payne was in a good mood when we knocked on his door. He barked "Enter".

"Just the two people I've been looking for," he said, motioning for us to close the door and sit down. "Now who can tell me what the hell is going on with your case." His eyebrows pulled together.

I gave him a short version of what we had been up to, the places we had visited, and witnesses we had interviewed.

"Okay," Captain Payne said, signing a document on his desk. "Who is leaking information to the press?" He arched a bushy eyebrow.

Officer Graham and I glanced at each other then back at Captain Payne. "No idea, sir, but we'll be careful what we share," I said.

"Good," he said. "Solve this quickly. And speak with no one but me. Understood?"

"Yes, Captain," we said.

Chapter Thirteen

THE LODGE

Detective Steve Campbell

There were still many people we needed to interview but stopped at The Lodge first, considering Daniel had set it up already. We entered The Lodge and headed for the conference room where everybody waited for us.

Officer Graham entered the hall first and introduced himself to everyone, then I did the same. Large eyes stared back at me, followed by uncomfortable coughs and a clearing of throats.

To save time, and Daniel money—he didn't have to close The Lodge—we agreed to meet everyone here in order for those to get to their shifts on time. It was also a good way for us to see how everyone behaved being in such close quarters once we asked uncomfortable questions.

Each interviewee sat at a table a short distance away from the other. Officer Graham took those on the left while I had the rest on the right, which included Daniel.

Julian Holmes had black receding hair, and his forehead glowed. His collar was too small for his thick neck, forcing him to leave the top button undone. He leaned on the table with his muscular arms, his meaty hands fisted.

"What do you do here?" I asked.

"I'm a bartender, like Brian." He nodded in Brian's direction.

"How long have you worked here?"

"About fifteen years."

"Did you ever see this woman?" I asked, showing him a picture of Ella.

"Yes, she'd been here many times. I've served her many drinks."

"Who was she here with?"

He cleared his throat and stole a glance at Daniel.

"Nobody will know who said what, Mr. Holmes, you have my word. I'd like to understand who our victim was, who her friends were, and what happened to her."

"She saw Daniel often in his office, but she also came here with the others."

"Do you know their names?"

"No, sir."

"Do you think she was a prostitute?"

He shook his head. "No, sir, she didn't come across as such. She was flirty with men, but it seemed she just wanted to keep them company, you know? They weren't the most handsome of men, so one would assume they were lonely."

"The men were married."

"That don't mean nothing, sir. They could've still been lonely," he said. I couldn't argue with him there. I understood why some men would go this route, but I needed to understand who Ella was and what exactly she did for these men.

"And they gave her money to keep them company?"

"Can't say, sir. I saw them give her presents; jewelry, clothing, and I overhead one say they wanted to take her to a spa for the day."

Apart from the promise ring Kevin had given her, if they had bought her jewelry, we found none in her room. Unless that was another lie Jessica had told us, and she had taken the items to sell.

"Can you remember the day when everyone saw her body in the open field?"

"I still have nightmares," Julian said, glancing at his hands. "She looked like a doll cut into two pieces. Whoever had done that was angry. He wanted to hurt her, embarrass her, defile her." He looked up at me. "I remember the day like it was yesterday. We were there," he jerked his chin at the others, "Daniel was there. It looked like he was crying. The officer who was there told us to get back, pushing us farther away. Then the van came and took her away. I don't recall seeing the officer taking down statements or pictures, but he could've done that before I arrived."

"Is there someone who was there you never saw before?"

Julian cocked his head to the side. "I don't know. I think it was just us. We all walked there and back together." He glanced at his watch. "If there's nothing else, I need to go, my shift is about to start."

"Here's my card," I said, handing it to him. "Call me if you remember anything else."

"Will do."

I sat at the next table. "Morning Grace," I said, handing her my business card. "Does everyone get on with Daniel?"

Grace's eyes widened as she glanced at Daniel. "He's our boss. We have to get on with him."

"Not necessarily."

She swallowed hard. "He's very strict and likes things done a certain way. And if one of us disobeys him, we get punished."

"How?"

"Fewer shifts mean fewer wages."

I glanced at Daniel, and he was already staring at me, then he turned his gaze onto Grace. I doubted he liked we were here speaking with his employees, but I didn't care. We had a case to solve, and if it involved him, we had to know everything.

"Did you see this woman around The Lodge?" I held up a photo of Ella.

"Yes, sir," she said, quickly glancing away and then at Daniel. "She was with him often," she whispered. "He bought her gifts, and she always used the exit near his office to come and go. She rarely used the front door when visiting him."

"Was he the jealous type?"

She shrugged. Her eyes darted to Daniel then back to me. "I don't think he's the jealous type. He isn't violent but he does have a temper. I'd never seen him raise a hand or yell at her. But when it comes to his staff and we don't do things perfectly he threatens us."

"What do you mean by that?"

"We basically have to do what he says, not complain about it, or we can find other work. I've never seen his wife, but I heard via the grapevine she's worse than him. It wouldn't surprise me if she wears the pants in his house, then he comes here and takes it out on us." She scoffed.

One thing I loved about these types of interviews was I could get a good picture of the person we were discussing.

If Daniel's wife behaved as Grace described, it could explain why Daniel was so unhappy.

"What do you think of the victim?"

"She was sweet, you know. Wouldn't hurt a hair on your head, but she hung around bad company. When I saw her that day, I felt sad for her. She was young, beautiful, had men at her feet, but it seems one of them didn't like what she was doing and took it out on her. To do that to her body is just," she choked on her words, and swallowed hard, "awful."

"Thank you for your honesty, Grace. Is there anything else you can think of? Who were the men she was with? Did anyone threaten her?"

"She saw Daniel, Charlie Roberts, Kevin Price, and Stanley something. He took over the surgical equipment business near the post office. And I heard there was another guy, but I never saw him, so not sure if he was a regular *friend* or not." She shrugged, then glanced at Daniel, who was staring at us again. "None of what I tell you will get to him?"

"No, what you tell me is between us, and the investigation, of course."

"Okay, good, because I need this job."

"How long have you worked here?" If I had to guess, Grace was in her mid-thirties with fine wrinkles and wore makeup sparingly. What made her seem old was her uniform; it was unflattering at best but a necessity.

"About fifteen years," she said, smiling kindly. "Started here when I turned nineteen. I've worked here almost as long as Daniel has."

"Who managed the place before Daniel?"

"Before, it was his grandfather. His father died in a

horrific hunting accident, so his grandfather left it to him when he turned twenty-four. His brother didn't like that and as far as I know, they hardly speak." She shrugged.

"Do you know when the others started working here?"

"Shortly after I did," Grace said, glancing around. "Yeah, a couple of years after I did. We've all been here for years and although Daniel is hot under the collar, he pays us well, but we work hard for it."

"Thanks for chatting with me," I said, glancing at my watch. Grace's shift started shortly after Julian's.

"Can I go?"

"Sure," I said, standing up and heading for the next table.

Daniel Hanson was next on my side. Officer Graham was still busy with his second interview; their conversation seemed intense.

"Mister Hanson," I said, sitting down. "We meet again. Thank you for arranging all this for us."

"It's the least I could do, or you would've dragged everyone down to the station. This way it's cheaper. Coffee?" He pointed at the urn on the table beside us.

"No thanks," I said, opening my folder with the photos. "You have answered some questions, but you left out the part where you dated the victim."

He raised both hands. "I know what this looks like, but I didn't want you to think I did something to her. I knew about the other men in her life, but when she was alone with me, she made me feel like the only man in her world. She was special. She was a gentle soul and when you find the man who did this, I'd love to hurt him. He took away the woman I loved."

This was something I could never understand; why hide the truth? It always came out. Daniel looked guiltier now than if he had just come out and told us about his relationship with Ella. Never mind saving us time wasted from running around looking for answers.

I exhaled a frustrated breath. "Did your wife know about her?"

"Stephanie didn't do this," he said, enunciating each word. "She knew about Ella. She knows about all the women I've dated. We have an arrangement. She tells me who she's with and I do the same. My wife had no reason to hurt Ella."

It seemed like a common theme; *open marriages*. I could never do that to Alice and I would hate seeing her with another man. I don't have a strong enough stomach to venture into these dark, carnal territories, because in my mind someone would get hurt.

"Did any of the men Ella dated want to hurt her?"

"Some were jealous, but I can't think of any who would do that to her." He swallowed hard. "She was a beautiful person, Detective. I should've been there for her. I should've protected her."

It seemed Daniel's guilt was enough punishment to last any man a lifetime.

"Why didn't you tell us the truth?"

"Because it looks bad," he said, combing his fingers through short hair. "When I saw it was Ella lying there in that field, it made me sick to my stomach. It was awful someone did that to her."

"And you know of no one angry enough to do that to her?" I pressed again. Sometimes asking the same question differently gave a better response.

"No, I wish I knew though, because I would make them pay."

"Did your brother know her?"

"Yes, everybody knew her."

"Where is he? I'd like to ask him some questions."

"Traveling the world, Detective. And he was nowhere near Ketchum the night she was murdered."

Chapter Fourteen

THE OTHERS

Detective Steve Campbell

"They all said the same thing," Officer Graham said, flipping through pages of his notebook. "They said Ella saw three or four guys weekly, they showered her with money and gifts, some took her away for weekends and they didn't know who was jealous enough to kill her." He tapped on his notebook. "Brian Smith said he noted bruising on her the week before her death but said nothing. He said Ella seemed scared. And when I pressed him for more information, he got up saying he was late for his shift."

"I wonder what happened?" I said, pouring sugar into my coffee. I wasn't supposed to have any, but today I needed a boost. "We need to write a timeline of events leading up to her death."

"I'm on it," Officer Graham said, pulling out a larger sketch book. "Can you give me copies of your notes and then I will start on it?"

"Sure," I said, placing my notebook on the photocopier and made copies. I handed them to him and enjoyed another sip of too sweet coffee. "Did anyone mention who the fourth person was Ella saw? Grace had mentioned another man with her, but never again."

"Maybe things didn't work out."

"Maybe. Now all we need to do is find out who he is."

"How do we do that?" he asked.

"I don't know."

"Have you looked into Ella's mom's death?"

"I was going to do that today."

"I'll start on the timeline, add the witnesses, who the boyfriends were, and then the info on her parents once you're done."

I nodded and watched Officer Graham walk toward his desk. I closed my office door and pinched the bridge of my nose. Duncan Turner was yet to return my phone call, so I dialed his number again, left another message.

Jessica had given me the check Ella's mom's lawyer sent monthly, and I dialed the number stamped on it.

"Hello, Manner, Josh, and Klein. How may I help you?" A woman said. She had the softest voice I'd ever heard. A need to protect her overwhelmed me, and I wondered what she looked like.

"Uh, hi," I stammered. "I'm looking for a Mr. Klein, please."

"What's this in connection with?"

"I'm Detective Steve Campbell from Ketchum and I'm investigating a murder. I have a few questions only Mr. Klein can answer."

"Oh, one moment, please." There was a beep, then someone picked up.

"Klein, Manner, and Josh," a man said.

"Hi, I'm Detective Steve Campbell and I'm investigating the murder of Ella Turner. I'd like to understand more about her deceased mother's estate and the monthly check you send her."

"Oh, jeez, wait a moment," he said, followed by papers shuffling, him dropping the receiver and moaning an apology when picking up. "They found Nancy's body in the river. Apparently, she and the husband had one of their fights. Nancy sped away, lost control of her car, crashed through the barrier and into the water below. She died on impact. She left her small estate to her daughter."

"Can you tell me when this happened?"

"In 1989. Her father, Duncan, wasn't happy about this. He fought with us every day and demanded the estate go to him in one large lump sum. I knew about his alcoholism and refused. I had him arrested when he assaulted me. Although Ella's name was on the check, I knew her father made her cash it and give it to him."

"How much is the monthly check?"

"Not much, about five hundred dollars."

"That's still a lot of money for a fifteen-year-old," I said, thinking. "Did the amount increase monthly or is that the flat rate?"

"Flat rate, which will cease once Ella passes away."

"What would happen to the rest of the money?"

"Nancy instructed it to go to charity." The silence stretched between us as I thought of how to tell him Ella had died five years ago. "Why are you asking these questions, Detective?"

"Someone murdered Ella Turner in 1997, Mr. Klein."

"Oh dear. Why are you only telling us now?"

"Unfortunately, she was a Jane Doe, and we left the case unsolved. Until now. I'll do everything in my power to find those responsible for her death."

Mr. Klein mumbled something to someone. "Thank you for letting me know, Detective. If she's been dead all this time, who has been cashing the check?"

"Her roommate because she thought Ella had run away with a boyfriend and would return."

He tsk'd. "The nerve of some people," he said. "I'll be stopping those checks immediately and paying the rest over to Nancy's selected charity."

"Good," I said. "Before you go, do you know how I can reach Duncan?"

"Of course. He still calls me monthly. Here is his number." Mr. Klein read the number to me, then ended the call.

I dialed Duncan's new number, and he picked up on the second ring. "What!" he roared, forcing me to move the receiver away from my ear.

"Is this Duncan Turner?"

"Yeah, who's this?"

"I'm Detective Campbell with the Ketchum Police and would like to inform you of the passing of your daughter."

He was silent for a long time.

"Mr. Turner?" I said, breaking the silence.

"When?"

"In 1997."

"What?" he said. "I don't understand. Are you sure? I mean, I've been getting the money from her every month."

The lines between my eyes deepened. I couldn't understand how that was possible. It sounded like Jessica had kept it all.

"Do you know a Jessica Wilkins?"

"I think so. She could be the one who phoned me some time ago, telling me she's Ella's roommate. She said Ella could only send half of the money."

It was possible Jessica kept up with the ruse so that Duncan didn't go to the police, or he'd known the lawyers would stop the checks if they knew Ella was dead and agreed to continue.

"Sorry for your loss, Mr. Turner."

"Is she the one who killed Ella?" Anger filled his words.

"We're yet to determine who murdered Ella."

"Why now if she died in 1997?" Duncan choked on his question. "Who hurt my only baby?"

"We could only identify Ella recently, but I assure you we're doing everything we can to bring the murderer to justice. Do you know of anyone who wanted to hurt her?"

"What? No! Who would hurt my baby? She was so young, so innocent. I mean, her life had just started," Duncan cried.

"Mr. Turner, would it be possible for you to come to Ketchum?" I wanted to look him in the eye when I asked him questions relating to his alcoholism and his arrest the day after his daughter's murder. I wanted to see if he had known and the only way to do that was to have him in front of me.

"Why?"

"Your daughter's body is still here, and we would like you to identify her." Dr. Brink had informed us that there were a handful of unclaimed bodies in her morgue and asked that we solve those, too. I told her we would get to it as soon as we could.

"Yeah, I'll think of something. It may take a while. I got to make some money first, but I'll be there."

"That's fine. Here's my number if you need to get hold

of me for any reason." I gave him my number and Officer Graham's in case he couldn't get hold of me.

"Thanks."

"You busy?" Officer Graham asked as I ended the call.

"Why?"

"James has some results for us."

Chapter Fifteen

RESULTS

Detective Steve Campbell

"That was quick," I said, standing beside James. We hovered around the table holding Ella's personal effects.

"It's been a slow week," James said. "I found Ella's fingerprints on everything, which is understandable, and I found a print belonging to a Mr. Kevin Price. He had his fingers all over the promise ring."

"Well, considering he was the one who gave it to her, I can understand that," I said, picking up the item with a gloved hand. "What about the diaries?"

"She wrote dark poems about love and death. Morbid stuff," James said with a shudder. "She mentioned four men; Daniel, Charlie, Kevin, and Stanley. I'm yet to discover who Stanley is, but I'm sure as the case progresses, you'll figure it out. She also mentions 'D', but I'm assuming it's Daniel."

"Thanks, James," I said, patting him on the shoulder. "Have you looked at her body again?"

"Dr. Brink is busy now."

"Speaking of Daniel," Officer Graham said, reading through his notebook. "Remember, I told you Brian Smith had noted bruises on her a week before her death," he said to me. "He also said Ella seemed scared to be alone with Daniel."

"You didn't tell me this."

"Yeah, sorry, I'm reading my notes now. She didn't want to see Daniel alone."

"After we speak with Kevin, we need to interview Daniel again."

Chapter Sixteen

STANLEY: THE WEEK BEFORE

Ella

"Jessica!" I yelled from my doorjamb. "Where's my blouse you borrowed last week?"

"I gave it back," she said, approaching. Her tone dripped with disdain. "I always give your stuff back, unlike you." She rolled her eyes. "Come, I'll show you."

Jessica opened my closet and pushed clothing on hangers one by one to the other side. When she didn't see my top, she sighed. "I'm sure I put it back." Her tone was gentler. "You probably wore it and now it's in the laundry. Have you checked the basket?"

"Let's check your closet," I said, heading for her room.

"Wait!" she yelled, running after me.

I hurried inside her room and opened her closet before she could. "Mine, mine, and this is mine," I said, grabbing my clothing. "And there is my blouse." I held the item in front of her, almost hitting her face.

"Yeah, well, at least it's clean."

"Stay out of my room, Jessica. I'm warning you. It's bad enough you overcharge me now you steal from me."

"I don't steal, you slut."

"Whatever," I said, clenching my jaw, and slamming my bedroom door shut. I hated living here. Unfortunately, until I got married or could afford a place of my own, I had to live here. Daniel had promised he'd help me find a place he'd pay for, but he'd been too busy. So, for now, I'd lock my bedroom door and hope it's enough to keep her out.

Slipping on the blouse, I tucked it into my pencil skirt. Then I secured the flower clip to the side of my head and applied eyeliner and lipstick.

Stanley was fetching me at seven and I wanted to be ready for him; I had five minutes left and quickly stepped into my heels. I flinched when the doorbell chimed, and Jessica's heavy footsteps passed my room.

"Hey Stanley," Jessica said. Her tone bordering on seductive.

"Where's my Ella?" Stanley said.

"She'll be right out." There was some disturbance and then... *"Don't you want the company of a real lady?"* she whispered, but I heard her.

I opened my bedroom door and slammed it shut, locking it. I tucked the key inside my purse. "Stanley!" I said, rounding the corner and stood beside Jessica, almost pushing her out of my way. "Just the gentleman I've been waiting for." I glared daggers at Jessica, who stepped away from me and averted her eyes.

"My darling," Stanley said, grinning. "I've waited all week to see your beautiful face." Stanley was a man of few words, but when he used them, he did so wisely.

"I've missed you," I said, slipping my arms around his waist for a hug. I felt the bulge in his pants press against my front, and I knew I would be in for a long evening with him. He was the only man in my life who could go at it all night long without tiring or hurting me.

"I've missed you, too," Stanley said, cupping my face. I rocked onto my toes and kissed him. He was the tallest and skinniest of my men, but the gentlest. His kind brown eyes always stared at me in wonder, and I couldn't help but smile shyly.

Jessica mumbled something, but I ignored her.

Stanley let me go and glowered at Jessica. "I heard that," he said. His tone was deep and throaty and filled with warning. "I'll do anything to protect Ella. Don't push me, Jessica." Then he turned to me and reached for my hand. "Let's go before I get angry."

"I didn't mean it," Jessica said in a high-pitched voice. "I'm like her sister."

"No, you're not, so stop pretending," I yelled. "I've locked my bedroom, and I'll know if you enter." I closed the door behind me, but not before seeing the hate in her dark brown eyes.

"Please consider moving in with me?" Stanley pleaded. "I will take care of you, you know this." He traversed down the stairs, gripping my hand like he was afraid I'd disappear.

I was fond of Stanley, but I didn't love him. The man I'd marry would be someone I loved and couldn't live without. At the moment, I could live without him. He was sweet, kind, and caring, but I didn't know if that was enough. I wanted to get out of that apartment, though.

"I'll consider your offer."

"It's all a man can hope for."

"What about your mother? Won't she mind?" That's the other thing to consider. I'd be living with her, too.

"She'll understand." Stanley led me to his car and

opened the passenger door for me. Once I was inside, he closed the door and knocked twice on the roof. He climbed in his side, closed the door, then turned to look at me. "The only reason Mother lives with me is because my wife died, and she didn't want me being alone. She wasn't ready for a retirement home then, but if you are mine and live with me, I'll see that it's just us. I make enough money to take care of you, Ella. Let me look after you."

His desperation filled the space between us, leaving me uncomfortable. I placed a calm hand on his thigh and squeezed. "I know you will, Stanley, and I'll consider your offer." I smiled kindly. He was a generous man, and I knew he would take care of me. But... "I've always been open and honest about the other men in my life," I said. "Therefore I need to let them know before I do anything."

Stanley squeezed the steering wheel, making it squeak. "I hate that you see them. Why can't you just see me?" His voice raised.

"We've gone over this, Stanley. It's the only way I can make ends meet, and I can't just dump them." I sounded as annoyed as I felt. In the beginning, each man only contributed financially to my life, but as time moved along, my feelings for them grew to a point where I wouldn't be able to give them up without a fight. I cared deeply for them, loving them individually.

"What if you came to work for me?"

"At your practice?"

"Yes, sure. I always need help. My current assistant is going on maternity leave and I'll need someone to fill her space. I'll pay you double that other schmuck was paying you at his business."

"He isn't a schmuck."

"I rescued him from going bankrupt."

"And he'll forever be grateful." I sighed. "If it wasn't for him we wouldn't have met."

"I know," he said, staring out of the window. "I know we each mean something different to you. I just wish it was us." He turned to look me in the eye, his feelings for me were evident in his expression.

I didn't like where this conversation was going and needed to change the subject. "I understand your perspective, but right now I can only consider your offer," I said, smiling. "Now," I reached for his hand, "enough talk about all this serious stuff. How about you and I have some fun?"

Chapter Seventeen

Ella

Diane Roberts entered the room wearing only heels. I shifted uncomfortably in my seat and flinched when Charlie wrapped his arm around my shoulders, pulling me closer to him.

"It's okay. Diane wants to play with us tonight."

"She's never wanted to before," I said nervously. "Why now?" I whispered. The last thing I wanted to do was upset Diane.

Diane stared at me as she entered the room, making her presence known. The woman scared me when she wore clothing, now that she was naked it left me feeling even more rattled. She and Charlie saw other people and sometimes saw others together, but since Charlie and I had been seeing each other, she never once suggested she play with us.

"Bring her here, Charles," Diane commanded.

"Come," Charlie said, reaching for my hands.

Tears welled in my eyes. "What does she want to do?"

"It will be fun, so relax." Charlie rubbed my shoulders and kissed my neck, sending goosebumps down my spine. He removed my top, forcing me to lift my arms above my head, but stopped with the material near my wrists and tied a knot. The bottom part of my top covered my face, blocking my view of Diane. I flinched when icy hands touched my breasts. "Shh, it's okay," Charlie said near my ear. "She'll be gentle with you."

I swallowed my fear and nodded; I could trust him.

I flinched when something heavy and cold closed around my wrists, forcing me to look up; shackles. A blindfold covered my eyes, and I tried shaking them away, but Charlie possessively held my neck in place.

"It's okay, my delicate little flower. You know I'll never hurt you. Trust me." He kissed my shoulder. I nodded. He secured the blindfold, taking away my sight.

Diane's smaller, much colder hands reached for my skirt. Her fingers danced between the fabric and my skin until she found the zipper at the back, opening it and allowed the material to fall to the ground.

"She's beautiful, Charlies," Diane said. "Even her pussy is petite and waiting to blossom for me."

There was a quick tug near my left-hand side. They exchanged whispered words, followed by a grunt. Then her icy hands were on my pelvic area and inside my panties.

"You're so wet," Diane said near my other ear. "I'm going to enjoy pounding that tight pussy and ass of yours."

Diane ripped my underwear from my body as she spun me around to face the other way. Charlie forced my legs apart and tied my ankles each to a table leg. Then bending my body forward so that he could tie my shackled wrists to the top of the table. My naked body pressing hard against the solid wood with little room to move my head or arms.

The events that happened next was a blur of pain.

Diane used device after device on my body; inserting them one by one, then two at the same time. She was not gentle as Charlie had promised, nor was she kind. No one had ever violated me like that before and I cried the whole time.

Charlie's hands held mine the entire duration of the assault; his fingernails digging into my flesh as he watched his wife rape me over and over again. I cried out many times for her to stop, but nobody heard or cared, and Charlie didn't stop it. It was as if Diane was trying to prove a point to me that I could never fully have Charlie all to myself. She wanted to violate me and put me in place; that she was the boss of me, my body, and Charlie.

When she was done with me, she slapped my bum hard, no doubt leaving a red welt. She removed my blindfold and smiled when she saw my tears. "Never think I don't know what goes on between the two of you," she pointed at me and Charlie, "I provide for him, and I will take away. You are nothing but a cheap whore he pays to fuck and to suck his limp dick. You will never get a dime more than what you're worth, so don't bother trying. If I hear you asking for more than the weekly allowance I provide my husband, next time I won't be so gentle."

"That's enough, Diane," Charlie said through tears, untying my hands. "Enough, babe, please. You've done enough damage, and she's learned her lesson."

"The same goes for you, too, Charles," she pointed her red-painted fingernail at him, "or I'll strap you to my table next. And I'll go to town on that pink ass of yours."

Charlie flinched as if she had slapped him.

Diane's heels clicked against the marble floors as she exited the room, slamming the door behind her.

"Oh, my gods, Ella, I'm so sorry," Charlie cried, untying my ankles. "I didn't think she was going to be so rough. I'm so sorry. Jesus, what did she do to you."

I said nothing. My body and mind were numb. The love I held for Charlie evaporated the moment Diane laid her hands on me, and in its place, hate unfurled itself.

Once I was free of all restraints, I stood, but my legs were too weak to hold my weight, and my knees buckled. Charlie caught me and carried me to the bathroom.

"Let me clean you," Charlie said. His face was red, his eyes filled with tears, and his body shaking. "I'm so sorry," he repeated over and over. He carefully placed me in the tub and ran warm water at first, then hot water to heat my body. My teeth chattering as I shivered from the sudden drop in my core temperature.

Charlie took his time cleaning me. He fetched bottles of water and food from the kitchen and fed me while I rested in the bath. My movements were robotic while my brain shut down, no doubt protecting me from what had just happened.

It felt like hours had passed. Charlie cried the entire time he cared for me, ensuring I was well fed, hydrated, and my body clean.

When my muscles stopped aching, and the blood stopped pouring out of me, I managed to climb out of the bath feeling less like an animal and more of a human.

Warm clothing waited for me, and Charlie helped me dress. "She's sorry for being so harsh," Charlie said, zipping up the front. "She's never provided clothing to any of the women before."

"Has she done this to all the women you've seen?"

"Yes, but never this bad," he said, averting his eyes. "It was always pleasurable to watch and then the girl would watch me fuck Diane, but not tonight. My cock wouldn't work after seeing all that blood." Charlie broke down again, tears staining his shirt. "I don't know what got into her."

"I never asked for more money, Charlie," I said as a tear betrayed me and slipped down my cheek; my numb body slowly awakening. "Why would she think that?"

"I asked her for more money because I wanted to surprise you with a gift, and I told her that. I told her you didn't know. It was going to be a surprise for you." He shook his head as if expelling thoughts. "I don't know what came over her. She's never been jealous of me." He wiped his face with the back of his hand. "You must believe me, Ella. I never wanted you hurt. I have feelings for you."

"Maybe that's why." My tone sounded hollow, emotionless. "She knows you care deeply for me, and she was teaching *you* a lesson. Don't fall in love with your fuck buddy." My tone now harsh and filled with hate.

I wanted to go home.

Charlie stood back and stared at me like I grew horns. He blinked but remained silent. He glanced over his shoulder, making sure the door was still closed, and rubbed his face. "I can't believe it, but you may be right. She was teaching *me* a lesson; I couldn't have feelings for anyone but her. Christ. I was so stupid." He turned toward me and fell to his knees. "Please forgive me, Ella. I promised that nobody would hurt you, and that's exactly what I've gone and done. You've lost all trust in me now, but I'll make it right if it's the last thing I do."

A heavy sigh escaped my mouth as more tears fell from my eyes. I combed my fingers through his hair. I wanted desperately to pull his hair out and dig my fingers into his eyes for being so stupid, but I couldn't do it. It wasn't his fault entirely. Besides, I could never hurt my Charlie; he was my cuddly teddy bear, and I cared deeply for him. From the moment I met him in his restaurant, I knew he'd always be my cuddly Charlie.

Pain seared through my body, reminding me of what had happened tonight, and I didn't want to see him ever again. That it was over between us. That Diane had finally gotten what she wanted; me out of his life.

Charlie stared at me with a pained expression. I didn't have to ask how he felt; I could see it on his face. He hated Diane as much as I did.

No. I couldn't allow her to win. She was not a nice person and she couldn't have Charlie all to herself. As much as I was hurting now, I knew myself. I couldn't reject him; I couldn't throw him away. I could never ignore him no matter how badly I wanted to hate him.

"It's okay, Charlie," I said, bending down. I cupped his face and crouched in front of him, wincing when pain shot into my pelvic area. "Ah," I moaned.

"Are you okay?" Charlie asked with concern.

"I'll be okay. My body will heal. It's my heart I'm worried about," I whispered. "I care deeply for you Charlie. Please don't hurt me again."

Chapter Eighteen

THE MOTEL WITH KEVIN: THE NIGHT BEFORE

Ella

"Where did all this money come from, Ella?" Jessica asked, counting every dollar.

"That money should be enough for the next two months," I said, placing the remaining cash into my purse.

"You must've fucked him real good," she said, not knowing it was hush money from Diane. She had come to her senses and felt bad for violating me, begging me for forgiveness. What she didn't know I'd taken pictures of the assault, even though Charlie had cleaned the evidence away. And I'd hidden my diary entry with the polaroids in case anything happened to me.

"My mom's estate pays me a monthly check," I said, wanting to end the conversation. "And they gave me a little extra." It was a lie, but greedy Jessica didn't have to know the truth.

"When did your mom pass away?"

"When I was young," I said, heading to my room. My

mom's estate would send me a check every month for the rest of my life. My great-grandfather made his money from selling his newspaper and the money grew year after year, leaving my mom a small fortune. Unfortunately, she drove herself into a river after she fought with my father; who till today thought it was unfair she had left me everything. But every month I sent him most of the money anyway. I knew he drank it away, or paid for sex, but after his work injury, he hadn't been able to find a job and the check wasn't enough to cover both of us, so I still needed to work.

"It's a pity you can't live off that money alone then you didn't have to sell your body."

I ignored Jessica's remark because it was futile explaining to her what the relationships with my men were like, and instead slammed my bedroom door closed. I wasn't in the mood to deal with her today.

My body still ached from my ordeal with Diane and was grateful I had no dates scheduled. All I wanted to do was rest and eat and sleep.

The doorbell chimed, and Jessica skipped to the door and opened it. They exchanged words I couldn't hear, then Jessica yelled. "Ella, it's Kevin."

The Roadside Inn was off the main road, surrounded by forest trees with a lake running behind it. It was a treat coming here with Kevin.

I was deep in thought, flinching when Kevin reached for the back of my neck and kissed me on the forehead. "What was that for?" I asked, smiling up at him.

"I'm lucky to have you in my life," he said, letting me go and leaning back in his chair.

"Are things bad at home?" I asked.

"Yeah," he said sadly. "After the accident, things have gotten worse. We don't speak even when we're in the same room." He raised a shoulder. "That's why I had to see you tonight."

"Luckily I was home alone."

He pursed his lips. "More wine?" he asked, changing the subject and lifting the wine bottle.

"Sure," I said, pushing my empty glass closer.

Kevin filled my glass and then his. "I want you to stop seeing the others," he said. His tone was deep and throaty, making all the hairs on my body stand up. He had a way about him, almost primal. His demeanor hinted at danger, but he offered nothing but pleasure. And although his request was selfish, I knew he wouldn't give an ultimatum; he wouldn't ask me to choose for fear of losing me.

"Give me a good reason," I said, reaching for my glass and enjoying a long sip; the liquid burning down my throat. "You're married Kevin. Why should I give up the others? I understand what you're going through and why you can't divorce your wife, but that doesn't mean I must give up my men. I can't throw any of them away."

He sighed. "I know. It's just," he left his sentence hanging and rubbed his face, "it's complicated."

"Well, so is my life. All of you want me to leave the others, yet none can commit to me. How am I supposed to feel?" I leaned back in the seat and folded my arms. Shifting uncomfortably, I flinched when pain shot up my one bum-cheek. I didn't want to leave the apartment tonight, but Kevin had asked so nicely to see me, saying he missed me and wanted to spoil me. But now, I regretted coming out.

After a long silence, I spoke, "Maybe you should take me home—"

"No!" he yelled, slamming his glass onto the table, spilling some wine. Shadows played on his face, twisting his features, and scaring me. I'd never seen him this angry before and was glad I was in a restaurant full of people. I glanced around, but nobody paid us any attention. I closed my eyes and enjoyed my wine. Even though Kevin was possessive, he wouldn't hurt me, and I wouldn't allow his outburst to ruin our evening.

After a few moments, his shoulders sagged slightly. He exhaled frustratingly. "Please, my darling," he said tenderly. "Let's not fight. Please spend the night with me and I'll take you home in the morning. Okay?" He reached for my hand, kissing the top gently.

I stared into his green eyes for the anger I had just witnessed, only finding sadness. "Okay," I said, smiling, but it didn't reach my eyes. This was the first time he'd flown into such a rage. It left me feeling uncomfortable. "I think tonight we sleep in our own bed."

"No, my darling, please," he said, taking my hand in his again. "Please, I need your warm body against mine now more than ever. No sex just cuddles. Please. I beg of you."

"Fine," I said, relieved we were no longer fighting or angry with each other; I hated it. "No funny business, mister." I smiled. "Now, what are we eating for dinner?"

A phone call from Kevin's wife interrupted dinner. She wasn't feeling well and demanded he return home immediately. He apologized profusely, paid for dinner, and gave me the keys to the motel room.

"I'm sorry," Kevin said, cupping my face and kissing me chastely. "I'll make it up to you, I promise." He said this every time he cut our dates short, and I honestly stopped caring, but I'd never say that to his face.

"It's okay," I said as sweetly as I could. There was no point making him feel bad; the look on his face said it all. And if he wanted to waste money on a motel room, it was his problem. "Go be with your wife. She obviously misses you. I don't know why you need me."

"It's complicated," he said, letting me go.

"It's only as complicated as we make it. Anyway," I said, cutting the conversation short; the evening was taking its toll on me and I wanted to sleep. "Thanks for dinner and the motel room. I'll enjoy it without you." I shook the key.

"Think of me." He grinned.

"Always," I said, reaching across the table for my leftover pasta in its takeout container. "I'll enjoy the rest of my evening binge watching The Practice."

Kevin smiled. "Maybe next week we can go to that fancy restaurant you keep telling me about?"

"It's a date."

I walked with Kevin to his vehicle and watched him climb inside. As he reversed out of the parking, I waved.

"Hey darling," a man said behind me.

I flinched and spun around. My heart racing in my chest. "What are you doing here?"

"Looking for you."

Chapter Nineteen

FINDING KEVIN

Officer Graham

Kevin Price was a hard man to track down. The details we had sent us to a warehouse that was in the process of closing. The owner confirmed Kevin had worked here years ago and wasn't sure whether the home address he had was valid, but he gave it to us, anyway.

Detective Campbell parked the car in the street. The front lawn had knee high grass and weeds, and two cars in the driveway.

"Come," Detective Campbell said, climbing out of the car. "Let's see if he's home."

I rang the doorbell while Detective Campbell stood beside me, writing in his notebook.

"We need to go to Dr. Brink after this," he said, closing his notebook.

"Do we have to?" I cringed the moment the words left my mouth. I hated coming across as weak, but I hated going there. It was something I still couldn't stomach.

"Yes." The lines between his eyes deepened. "She'll be going over our victim's autopsy and showing us her body. You need to attend."

"Okay," I said with a shudder, grateful I hadn't eaten yet. The last thing I needed now was throwing up with the detective watching me. "I've never heard of them keeping a body for so long."

"Yeah, apparently, they'd forgotten she was even there. When they checked to see what had happened to her body, they realized their mistake."

"I suppose that's a good thing for us, then."

"Yeah, and before I forget," Detective Campbell continued, "I found something in the footage you gave me." A nervousness settled in my bones. "And I'd like for you to take a closer look."

"Are you referring to the video where an officer removes the evidence from Jack Haskins parent's box?"

"Yep, that's the one." He didn't look at me when he answered.

He knew something and wanted to rattle me; it was working. I couldn't believe I was so stupid. It all happened around the time Macey had lost her job, and we desperately needed money for Stacey. When Jack offered me more than enough to pay off all our debt and enough to live comfortably for the rest of the year, I couldn't say no, but now my deed had come back to bite me in the ass. First it was my father and his ties to drug dealers, then killing himself, and now this. I had nobody but myself to blame for ruining my career.

I flinched when the door creaked open. "What?" A woman said, opening the door wide enough to see one side of her face.

"Mrs. Price?" I asked, glancing down at her and grateful for a change in subject.

"Yeah, who are you?"

"I'm Detective Campbell," he said, showing her his I.D. I did the same. "We're here to speak with your husband."

"Kevin!" she yelled. "The cops are here." She opened the door wider and stepped to the side. "I'll bring some coffee." She disappeared into the dark house.

"Jeez Marjorie, put some lights on," Kevin yelled, running down the stairs. He switched on the light, illuminating the foyer. "Hi, what's the problem?"

"Do you remember a woman named Ella Turner?"

Kevin paled and quickly stepped outside, closing the door behind him. "Please, she can't hear any of this. Yes, yes, I knew Ella. Did you find out who killed her?" He approached the swing on the veranda and sat down. "Please sit."

"Did you kill her?" Detective Campbell said, catching me by surprise. He'd never been that direct with a potential suspect before.

"No, Detective. I loved Ella. Why would I hurt her?"

"Because you wanted her all to yourself. If you couldn't have her, nobody can."

"No," Kevin said, shaking his head. "I didn't like the fact that she saw the others, but I'd never hurt her. Ever. I wanted nothing but to protect her."

"Did your wife find out about you two and hurt her?" Detective Campbell said.

Kevin was quiet for a moment, then shook his head. "No, never. What they did to Ella was vicious, and that person had to have the strength and the space to do it. Marjorie comes across as harsh, but in reality, she's as timid as a little bunny. She wouldn't hurt a fly. Besides, did you see how short she is?"

"Anything is possible," Detective Campbell said.

I made notes in my book.

"Here you go," Marjorie said, opening the front door with her free hand and carried a tray with the other. "We only have black coffee," she said, wincing, then quickly held the tray with both hands. "I need to go to the store for milk. Should I go now, honey? I don't mind."

"Yes please. You know I only drink coffee with milk in it." Kevin smiled up at her, but I noticed the nervousness in his eyes.

Marjorie sighed. "Okay, I'll be back in five." She entered the house and was out again in seconds, holding her handbag and car keys.

"Was Ella the only woman you saw on the side?" I asked, feeling like I needed to add more to the interviews instead of leaving all the heavy lifting for Detective Campbell. The last thing I needed was for him to go to Captain Payne and tell him he didn't need me working with him anymore.

"Ella was the one and only woman I saw on the side. Marjorie and I were going through a very difficult patch with no end in sight. After Ella's murder, we patched things up, and I had no one else."

"What would your wife do if she found out now?" Detective Campbell said.

"She'd kick me out. She might be submissive, but she's an unforgiving woman, Detective. If she knew anything, I'd be homeless. That's why I find it hard to believe she would do anything to Ella. She would take it out on me, not the other woman."

"Do either of you work?" Detective Campbell said.

"I'm in sales," he pointed at the logo on his golf shirt, "but they pay little. Marjorie comes from money and is a stay-at-home wife."

"Do you have any children?" I asked.

"Our son passed away in 1996." Kevin glanced down at his coffee cup; his thoughts lost. His dark, thinning hair had started to lighten on the sides, and the hard lines near his green eyes showed his age. Otherwise, he seemed fit and healthy. He wore neatly pressed tan trousers and a golf shirt with his company's logo for medical supplies.

"Is that when things became strained at home?" Detective Campbell asked compassionately.

"Yes," Kevin said, glancing up. "A car hit him when he ran into the road to fetch his ball. It was an awful time, and I don't want to relive it."

"That's fine," Detective Campbell said. "Can you tell us if there was anyone who wanted to hurt Ella?"

"No, I mean the other men all wanted her to choose them, but we were all married and none wanted to leave their wife. So, we were all stuck."

"And the promise ring you gave her?" I asked. "What was the promise?"

"That I would leave Marjorie." He visibly sighed. "But I couldn't dump her after our son died. That was cruel. And I felt terrible not keeping my promise with Ella."

"But having an affair with a woman you weren't planning on marrying wasn't cruel?" Detective Campbell said, anger rolling off his words.

"I know, I know," Kevin said, holding his free hand up in mock surrender. "I suck as a man, but I was torn between the current and the future, leaving me with the unknown. It was difficult for me."

"Is this you in the photograph?" Detective Campbell held up the photo we got from the Roadside Inn desk clerk.

Kevin took it from his hands and nodded. "Yes," he said, choking on his word. "Sorry, I'd forgotten about this." His hands shook as he stared at it.

"You're holding her possessively. Care to respond to that?"

"I wasn't having a good evening and didn't want her out of my sight. She was intoxicated, and I didn't want anything bad to happen to her."

"When was the last time you saw her?"

Kevin handed the photo back and glanced away.

"Kevin?" Detective Campbell said.

Keven glanced at him. "Before you accuse me of anything," he said nervously. "I saw her the night she was murdered. We ate dinner together, but before I could take her to the Roadside Inn, my wife demanded I come home. I gave Ella the key to the room, and I left her there. Alive." He wiped tears away. "You must believe me. I could never hurt her. Someone else was there after I left and took her away from me."

"Who?"

"Believe me, if I knew, he'd be dead," he said. "I asked the clerk, I asked people at the restaurant next door, but nobody recalled seeing her with anyone." He shifted on the seat and reached for something in his pocket. "Look," he said, opening his wallet. "I still keep a photo of her. I miss her. I loved her."

We didn't stay long after that and neither of us drank the coffee. The rest of the interview was bland as he described the men, yet knew little about each of them, and we still knew nothing about Stanley or where to find him.

"Everything okay?" I asked.

"Yeah, why?"

"You seemed angry."

"I guess the case is getting to me," Detective Campbell said. "All these married men playing with the hearts and feelings of their wives and Ella. Kevin was right, it's cruel no matter which way you look at it."

"Yeah, you're right," I said, opening my car door. Perhaps the case was getting to me too.

Once we were in the car and back on the road, I thought of something. "Don't you find it strange that two men work in the hospitality industry and two work in the medical industry?"

Detective Campbell glanced at me, then back at the road. "What do you mean?"

"I don't know." I wasn't sure what I was getting at or if it was even connected; only that it seemed strange. "We know little about Stanley. Who is he? Is he the one who owned the device company Ella had worked at and does Kevin work at the same medical device company as a salesman? Is that how they met Ella?"

"Hmm," he said. "It's intriguing for sure. We have time, let's go there now."

Chapter Twenty

SURGICAL DEVICES

Officer Graham

Detective Campbell drove the rest of the way in silence, and I couldn't help but stress. He was going to tell Captain Payne I took Jack's money and moved evidence. Captain was going to fire me. I made a stupid mistake, but that didn't mean they couldn't trust me. I knew I was wrong doing it, but we needed the money. And I'd accept the punishment. If I lost my job, I'd join a private security firm. An ex-colleague had connections I could reach out to.

I exhaled a nervous breath when Detective Campbell parked the car outside a dilapidated office block that was in the process of being refurbished. Across the road was the post office.

We climbed the flight of stairs and reached the only office on that floor. The sign on the door read 'Whitaker Devices'. Detective Campbell opened the door and greeted the mature woman sitting behind the reception desk.

"Morning, can I help you, gentlemen?" The woman

asked. Her glasses sat perched on the edge of her nose, and her short curly gray hair framed her aging face neatly. She wore a vintage pastel blue jersey that matched her light blue-colored eyes.

"Morning. Who owns this office?" Detective Campbell asked with a smile.

"Dr. Stanley Whitaker," she said warmly.

My back stiffened, and I glanced at Detective Campbell, but his attention was on the woman. At least we found Stanley and now we knew his last name, too.

"Is he in?"

"No, he's at his medical practice."

"What kind of practice does he run?"

"He's a surgeon," the woman said. My arms pebbled; maybe this was the connection we needed. Then the lines between her eyes deepened. "Who are you and what's this in connection with?" She glanced from Detective Campbell to me.

"Apologies," Detective Campbell said, raising his I.D. for her to see. "I'm Detective Campbell and this is Office Graham," he pointed at me, "and we would like to speak with Dr. Whitaker in connection with a murder."

"Oh, deary me," she said, reaching for the phone. "Would you like me to ask Dr. Whitaker to come here or would you prefer going to his practice?"

"Don't phone ahead," Detective Campbell said. "We would like to look around first, if that's okay. In the meantime, could you write the address of his practice on a piece of paper, and we'll go there?"

"Okay, s-sure," she stammered. She stood and unlocked the frosted glass door behind her. "He's an excellent surgeon, even makes his patients prosthetics himself instead of sending them elsewhere. He includes it in his price, of course. All the medical insurances love him for it because he gives a discount, and there have been no complaints against him."

"What does he do when there's a device he can't make himself?" Detective Campbell said.

"He brings the specialist here to make it. It's more about the patient's convenience than the money. Dr. Whitaker cares about his patient's wellbeing."

He sounded like the perfect doctor.

"Thanks, Ma'am," Detective Campbell said, entering the room first. "We won't be long."

Inside the large room, prosthetic arms and legs dangled from various chains connected to the ceiling with a work bench beneath them. The workbench had tools and plastic parts scattered everywhere. There was a locked glass cabinet on the left-hand side that held more expensive prosthetics, which included false eyes, and the electronics to move various hands and feet.

"As much as I understand the need for places such as this one, it still gives me the creeps," I said as a shiver went down my spine. I picked up an arm and the mechanical fingers waved at me. I flinched and dropped it.

"Yeah," Detective Campbell said, chuckling. "Me too."

"Doesn't look like there's much of anything else here," I said, walking between the workbench and the wall, ensuring there was nothing else needing to be searched.

"Here's a cabinet over here with already pre-made devices," Detective Campbell said, opening a metal locker.

"I wonder why he has a receptionist sitting here all day if she does nothing?" I asked.

"Let's ask her." Detective Campbell headed for the door. "Ma'am," he said, leaning on the reception counter. "How long have you worked for Dr. Whitaker?"

"I've been working for him since he opened this center," she said. When she smiled, it lifted her face, but also creased the loose skin. "I'm his mother, Detective," she said matter-of-factly.

Detective Campbell arched eyebrows. "Lovely to meet you, Mrs. Whitaker," he said, adding some charm. "You must be proud of him?"

"Yes, very," she said, her smile still reaching her tired eyes. "After his father passed away, I had a lot of time on my hands and Stanley needed help. This way I see him every day, and I stay busy."

"Were you young when you had him?" Detective Campbell asked. "You don't look a day over sixty."

Mrs. Whitaker giggled. "You're too kind, Detective. I'm almost seventy."

"Well, you look fabulous, Ma'am." He knocked twice on the counter. "We'll be on our way."

"May I ask whose murder you're investigating and why you need my Stanley?" She asked with concern etched on her face. Her smile gone.

"It's from a case that happened five years ago, Ella Turner's murder."

"Oh, deary me," she said with a gasp. "She was a lovely girl. I didn't know she had died."

"Did you know her well?" I asked.

Mrs. Whitaker looked at me for the first time. "No, son, I had only met her once or twice, and she seemed like a good girl. I never heard of her again."

"And you remembered her from then, even though you only met her a couple of times?" Detective Campbell asked.

"My memory is still sharp, Detective." She grinned. "My body is old, but my mind still works."

"I hope I age as gracefully as you," Detective Campbell said. "Thank you for your time. We'll be on our way."

"Tell Stanley I said hi and I'll make lasagna for dinner tonight."

Detective Campbell parked the car outside Dr. Stanley Whitaker's medical practice, and next door to it was a coffee shop. This building was two blocks away from his medical device office and across the road from the hospital.

We first bought ourselves a cup of coffee, then we went next door. All ten seats had bums on them, and there were two women working at reception. As we entered, they glanced up, but the girl on our left spoke first.

"Dr. Whitaker's, how can we help you?" Delores said. They each wore a pretty name tag.

"Morning," Detective Campbell said, placing his coffee on the counter. "I'm Detective Campbell and this is Officer Graham. We would like to speak with Dr. Whitaker." He leaned his elbows on the hard surface.

"Oh," Delores said, glancing at Maggie beside her, then at the appointment book in front of her. "He's busy."

"I understand," Detective Campbell said, glancing over his shoulder, then in a whisper said, "We can either see him now, or arrest him in front of his patients and drag him to the station." He showed her his I.D.

"You can see him when the patient he's with leaves," Maggie said, desperately trying to hide her anger. I didn't think she liked cops.

"Thank you, Maggie. We appreciate your help."

Detective Campbell smiled, picked up his coffee and

stood in the hallway to ensure we saw the various consulting room doors open and close.

Two minutes later, a door opened, and a smiling patient exited followed by a man wearing a white coat with piercing dark eyes. He stopped in the middle of the hallway, staring at us. I thought he was going to bolt like a racehorse out of the starting blocks.

Maggie entered the hallway and whispered something into the doctor's ear. "Thanks, Maggie. I'll take it from here." Then he looked at Detective Campbell. "Detective," he said, motioning for us to enter his consulting room and he disappeared inside.

"Thank you for squeezing us in," Detective Campbell said, sitting down.

I closed the door behind me and sat beside the detective.

"You're here about Ella?"

"Yes," Detective Campbell said. "How did you know?"

"I have my ways." He smirked.

"Your mom says she's making lasagna for dinner tonight."

Dr. Whitaker smiled, but he didn't seem pleased.

I took in my surroundings. There were three certificates on the wall proving he was a surgeon, specializing in replacing limbs with artificial devices. There was a wash-basin near an examination bed and a clothes rack that held a jacket and a fedora. I frowned. I knew there was something about that hat but couldn't place it.

"What was your relationship with her?" Detective Campbell asked, pulling me back to the interview.

"My wife had passed away years before I met Ella. After I qualified as a surgeon, I used the money she had left me and opened my practice and my device business. I preferred my patients had quality prosthetics and not these awful ones they could purchase from other countries or a pharmacy. Once established, I met Ella at The Lounge." Dr. Whitaker leaned forward on his desk. "There's one thing you need to understand, Detective. I loved her. I wanted to take care of her, even offered her a job in my practice. I'm sure she would've taken it if they hadn't murdered her. And when you find out who did this awful thing to her..." he left his threat hanging.

"Can you remember all the men in her life?" I asked, opening my notebook.

Dr. Whitaker glanced my way and leaned back in his chair. "Kevin Price, Daniel Hanson, Charlie Roberts, and another guy." He counted on his hand. "He's the one she first worked for. I bought my prosthetics company from him and worked through lawyers. I never met the guy. What's his name?" he snapped his fingers as he thought, "Daniel knows the guy, he introduced them still. What's his name?" He tsk'd. "Sorry, I can't remember but check with Daniel. He'll know."

"This is the first time we're hearing there's a fifth guy involved," Detective Campbell said.

"Yeah, speak to Daniel. He'll know more about it. I remember counting all the fingers on one hand when I asked her about them." He held up his large hand and wiggled his fingers. "Five."

The more we investigated this case, the more I was starting to hate Daniel. He lied from the beginning and now there could be a fifth guy involved and he had said nothing about him. Detective Campbell glanced nervously at me, then went back to questioning the doctor.

"There's a handful of men who work at medical device companies." He counted on his fingers. "Kevin Price works as a salesman for one, and you. Are you two in competition?"

"Heavens no, Detective. There are more than enough patients to keep all of us above water. Believe me, there was never any bad blood between us."

"Other than the girl."

"Yes, other than Ella. I asked her to marry me at least once a week and she always turned me down. She was afraid of hurting the others," he said sadly. "Unfortunately, I couldn't make an honest woman out of her."

"Was she a prostitute?"

"No," he retorted. "It was never about sex, and I don't think she always had sex with us every time we saw her. The two years I knew her, we only slept together a handful of times, and I always had to go slow. She was tiny down there and any guy with a dick larger than my middle finger would most certainly tear her." He raised his finger for us to see.

This was the first time anyone mentioned this, and I didn't recall seeing anything in the autopsy report. I made a note to ask Dr. Brink.

"Is there anything else you can recall during that time?" Detective Campbell said. "Was she scared of anyone? Who was the last to see her alive?"

Dr. Whitaker thought for a moment. "I had a date with her a week before she died, then it was Charles, then Kevin. It had to have been Daniel or that other guy. I'm sure of it. I phoned her, but her evil roommate was famous for not giving her messages."

"About that," Detective Campbell said, deep in thought. "What do you make of her roommate?"

"Jessica? Terrible person. She always stole Ella's cloth-ing, her money, blamed her for stealing her husband-to-be —" he rolled his eyes.

"Who was that?"

"Daniel, of course. But what Jessica failed to realize was Daniel was already married and he would never leave his wife. I met her once, the wife, and she's worse than Charlie's wife. That woman scares the crap out of me, Charlie's wife, that is. No wait, both of their wives scare me. If I was the last man on earth and I had to choose between the two of them, I would kill myself. I think they went to the same evil school."

This case was turning into something else, and I made a note that we had to speak with both men again and this time with their wives.

Chapter Twenty-One

THE WHITE DAHLIA

Detective Steve Campbell

Ella Turner's body had been in the cooler for five years and was perfectly preserved. Nothing had changed except the minutes and hours wasted by Officer Aldridge, who had buried her case under other cases and then he retired.

Her cold body was still in two pieces, with her scary smile reaching her ears. I couldn't fully comprehend what I was staring at. It was like my brain tripped in on itself.

Sometimes death did that to me. I would stare at a body and wonder what that person's mannerisms were like when they were alive. What did they sound like? Were they a decent human, and who did they touch with their light, ensuring everyone remembered them once gone? A person's soul animated the shell of a body; it helped them move around on earth. Without that shell, nobody could see them, touch their skin, or hear their words. With no soul, the body went back to nature. And depending on one's religion, the soul would go to heaven or be reincarnated; to return and hopefully do a better job next time around.

There was a smell in the air I couldn't quite place, but I knew it was death. The coppery smell of the body, mixed with the cold of the morgue, and possibly other elements to preserve her body. And in-between all that, a floral scent which may have been Dr. Brink's perfume, or it was the smell of the White Dahlia flower Ella used to wear behind her ear; the petals soaking into her skin forever.

Questions about my life swarmed my mind as I stared down at Ella's pale, smiling face, and I pictured Alice lying there. I didn't think I could carry on with my life like I did now if Alice were gone. Everything in my life would change. If the person with whom I'd shared my life with for over twenty years was gone, just like that, in an instance, it would devastate me. It would change me completely, forcing me to see life through grieving eyes, as I tried pushing the pain through a broken heart. I didn't think I could do it.

I blinked and Ella was there, waiting for us to discuss her body, her terrible murder, and the DNA traces we hoped were still on her body. I hoped somebody felt for her the way I felt for Alice.

I had empathy and compassion for others; putting myself in their situation to understand their perspective, and today I felt strange looking at Ella. Perhaps it was age or this case, or that I wanted to make sure she was really gone. Without thinking I touched her hard, cold cheek. Dr. Brink cleared her throat, and I knew she saw me. She probably wanted to ask if I was okay because I touched the victim. She said nothing and I was grateful for the quiet moment she offered.

I glanced up and smiled sheepishly. "Sorry about that,"

I said, reaching for the disposable gloves and pulling them on. "I shouldn't have done that."

Dr. Brink smiled warmly. "Lucky for you, I've already performed the second autopsy," she said with a wink.

I swallowed hard, feeling overwhelmed with emotion, and blinked back tears. "Did you find anything that was missed the first time?" I managed to say and exhaled deeply.

"Before I get to that," Dr. Brink said, pulling the sheet further down Ella's body, revealing how they had butchered her. I glanced up at her face instead, at the beauty mark near her left eye. I stared at her black hair, then her green eyes. Today she wore a silk purple blouse with a black pencil skirt, and her white coat over that. Dr. Brink reminded me of a gothic sex kitten, but I'd never say that out loud. If it wasn't for her morbid fascination with death, I was sure she'd be in a burlesque show or married to a rich CEO.

"Steve?" Dr. Brink said, waving a hand in front of me.

"Yes?" I asked, blinking at her.

"I was just saying I suspect the person responsible knew how to cut a body."

"What makes you think that?"

"They knew where to cut," she said gravely.

"Do you think it's a doctor?"

"Maybe, or someone who has an interest in surgery. They don't have to be a doctor, just someone with a steady hand and nerves of steel."

"Hmm, okay. And a strong stomach." I thought of Officer Graham.

"I also asked what your thoughts were behind finding a piece of her black top in the forest?"

"Oh, um," I stammered, trying to get a grip on the present moment; I had a job to do, and could dwell on my

thoughts when home. "I was wondering about that myself."
Clearing my throat, I continued. "The only thing I could
come up with is our killer took her there as a romantic
suggestion, a picnic under the moonlit sky before taking her
home and butchering her. We found it far from the hiking
trail, so it's possible that it stayed out there for so long
without being seen."

"I've brought in an I.T. specialist to check our system,"
Dr. Brink said with a look of annoyance on her face. "When
I matched the blood and fibers to the cold case, we got no
other results and missed her arrest for underage drinking.
Otherwise, she would've been identified earlier, saving you
time."

"I hope they find the error," I said, feeling concerned
about whether this happened often. "It angers me she
wasn't identified five years ago."

"Me, too, Detective."

Officer Graham paled and asked to be excused. He sat
in the corner chair, watching from a distance. I think he was
also stressing from the conversation I had with him
regarding that video; he understood I was on to him. I was
still deciding what to do about it, but I had to tell Captain. I
couldn't bury this, or I was no better than Officer Graham.

"He's not cut out for this part," Dr. Brink said.

"No, he's not," I added, stepping closer to the body.
"One of Ella's boyfriends had suggested all the men she had
dates with had below average size penises, and I was
wondering if you came to the same conclusion."

"Yes," she said, pulling the sheet completely off. "I'm
grateful we preserved Ella's body perfectly," she pointed at
the section where they had cut her in half, "like the original
autopsy I discovered they had sexually assaulted her anally,

and she has small genitalia. She's never been pregnant, and I found DNA on her eyelids."

"Eyelids?" I glanced at Ella. "Do you think he closed her eyes after he killed her?"

"He tried," she said, nodding. "But obviously they opened again because of secondary relaxation after rigor mortis." She pointed at Ella's legs. "He thoroughly cleaned her body but missed her eyelids and a spot near her hip bone." She smiled.

"I hope it's not some idiot who works here who touched her wearing no gloves."

"I hope so too. James is busy with it now, so we'll know soon."

"Okay, that will help our case once we get the results, and I hope it points us to the killer."

"Same, Detective," Dr. Brink said. "Are you feeling better now?" she asked. The intensity of her stare left me feeling slightly uncomfortable.

"Yes, why do you ask?"

"Just asking." Her green eyes pierced mine. "Just making sure you're okay. I've seen good cops buckle under pressure and end up hurt. I'd hate for the same thing to happen to you."

"Thank you for your concern, but I'm okay. I may take a long weekend sometime soon, you know, just to unwind a bit."

"That's a good idea. James is taking a few days off soon, and then myself. We all need downtime, Detective." She glanced at Officer Graham. "He may need something soon, too." She grinned.

Chapter Twenty-Two

IT'S A DATE

Detective Steve Campbell

The autopsy with Dr. Brink was the last thing we did for the day, and I couldn't wait to get home. I dropped Officer Graham off at the station and came right home. I brought the case file with me and would complete my report after dinner.

"Hey, honey," I said, snaking my arms around Alice and kissing her tenderly. I held on for longer than usual and Alice shifted uncomfortably in my arms.

"Are you okay?" she asked, distancing herself from me, forcing me to let her go, and glanced up at me. "Why do you look so sad?" She reached for my face and gently caressed my cheek. "What's wrong?"

I grabbed her hand and kissed it. "It's nothing. The day was long and," I kissed her hand again, "I missed you."

"Ah, honey, well," she said, beaming, "I made a casserole for dinner with a salad. I hope you're hungry."

"Famished."

After dinner, we sat in the enclosed porch on the swing with a glass of wine and enjoyed the evening sounds; the stridulating insects and croaking of frogs. It was an absolute delight listening in on their conversations, and I was glad it had stopped snowing.

I watched Alice smile and close her eyes. Her happiness brought sought after relief considering everything she had been through; the miscarriages and then the move from Las Vegas to Ketchum.

"I've booked a weekend away for us," I said, sipping some wine.

She smiled, opened her eyes, then turned toward me. "Oh," she said. Her eyes twinkling in the dim light. "Where are we going?"

"It's close. But there are no neighbors, so if we want to walk around naked all weekend we can," I teased.

She laughed; it was that laugh that shook her body because she was truly happy. "What will we get up to?" she said with a wink.

"Absolutely nothing," I said, sighing then smiling. "I'm sure we'll just sit around and knit, or maybe watch birds. Anyway, your birthday is next Saturday, and we'll be there from Friday morning all the way to Monday mid-morning. We'll take a slow ride and be back home by lunchtime."

"Thank you, hon," she said, her eyes glistening with unshed tears. "I think we need a weekend away where you don't work and I'm not constantly in my head. I'm looking forward to it."

I leaned over and kissed her chastely. "Me, too, babe. It's going to be wonderful. We can fish, light a fire, and there's even a hot tub for who knows what." I smirked. I hadn't looked forward to anything like this since we tried to fall pregnant. At least this time around, nobody would get hurt, and we'd leave the cabin refreshed.

Chapter Twenty-Three

DANIEL MISSING

Detective Steve Campbell

"Phillip," I said, catching his attention. "Is Daniel in?"

"No, Detective," Phillip said, closing the gap. "He hasn't been to work in two days."

"Has he done this before?" The lines between my eyes deepened.

"No, sir."

Phillip was about to leave when I called him back. "How have the staff been since we interviewed them?" I knew of at least one who seemed uncomfortable that Daniel was there, and another who saw bruising on Ella the week before she died. We needed to find out what had happened to her during the days leading up to her death, and I suspected Daniel knew more than he let on.

"It's all been normal," he said, raising a shoulder. "Daniel has been more preoccupied than normal. When you find him, you can ask him directly. If you'll excuse me, Detective, I have guests that need checking in."

"Thanks Phillip," I said. "Mind if I grab a coffee?"

"Sure, the bar is up ahead." He pointed toward the restaurant area.

I waited for Phillip to head in the opposite direction, then I traversed the hallway toward Daniel's office.

When I was sure nobody would walk in on me, I entered Daniel's office and locked the door. It looked the same as the first time I was here except the desk had papers strewn everywhere, like someone was looking for something.

I searched his desk drawers, but there was nothing but files, loose papers, elastic bands, name badges, and pens. I stood beside his chair and glanced around. A chilly feeling crept into my veins as recognition set in. When we were first here, I noticed the picture on the wall but didn't realize who it was. The black-and-white picture was of a naked woman leaning backwards on a couch; and now that I knew what Ella looked like when she was alive, the woman in the picture was her. Also, in the picture was something near her ear that might have been the white dahlia she wore in her hair.

I approached the framed black-and-white picture, took my phone out of my pocket and snapped a shot of it. There was a signature in the bottom right-hand corner with the initials 'DD'.

I flinched when my phone buzzed. Officer Graham had spoken with Marjorie about Kevin's whereabouts, and she couldn't remember it was so long ago, but said that they always spent their evenings together, so he had to have been with her. Officer Graham sent another text letting me know he didn't think she knew anything, and that Kevin was right. She was too small to carry a woman's body by herself.

I had sent Officer Graham to speak with Marjorie while Kevin was at work, and not to say anything else. It was up to Kevin whether he told her the truth about his extracurricular affairs.

I checked both sides of the hallway, closed the door quietly behind me, and hurried toward the exit. As I was leaving, a black SUV pulled up to the valet parking, and a man stepped out.

"Daniel," I said, closing the distance between us.

Daniel frowned.

"Can we talk about the picture in your office?"

Daniel's frown melted away, and a smile stretched across his face. "You've got me confused with my brother."

Confusion melted the words on my tongue.

"I'm David Hanson," he said, proffering a hand.

"Twin?" I said, confirming. His hand was dry and firm. We shook then he let my hand go.

"Yes," he said, chuckling. "Did Daniel not mention me?"

"Uh, no, he didn't," I stammered.

"That's only because I'm the handsome twin." When he smiled, his cheek dented, revealing a small dimple; the only difference between the two. "Do you know where Daniel is? I've been looking all over for him."

"No, I was about to ask you the same thing."

David started walking inside, and I hurried after him.

"Can we talk quickly?" I said, keeping up with his long strides. "Did you know Ella Turner?"

David stopped dead and scowled at me. "Yes, why? Do you know who the bastard is who killed her?"

"I'm Detective Campbell," I said, handing him one of my business cards, "and I'm working on her case. How well did you know her?"

David took my card and read it slowly before pocketing

it. "Daniel introduced us. I gave her a job and when that business folded, I photographed her."

"So, you're the one who signed the *DD* on the photo in Daniel's office?"

"Yes, she was a beautiful specimen. Whoever had hurt her deserves to be punished."

"We'll find the person," I said, as a surge of hope flooded my system. Perhaps David knew more. "What can you tell me about Ella, or anyone who might have hurt her?"

David leaned against the wall and sighed. "Ella had a heart of gold. At first glance, people assumed she was a whore. That she went after men with money so they could provide for her and pay for her services. But she was nothing like that. She accepted sad, broken men and gave them love, tenderness, and hope, and in exchange for that, yes, the men gave her money and gifts. But she never asked for any of it."

I nodded, making notes in my book.

"Daniel's wife beats him and leaves no traces on his body. Charlie's wife dominates him, and any girl he brings home. Kevin lost a child and almost lost his wife. Stanley's wife died, while his mother turned into Mrs. Bates. I gave Ella her first job here, then I lost the business because I couldn't manage it properly, and Stanley took it over, saving my ass. That's how he met Ella. Then I turned to photography, and she gave me the boost in my career. Without that boost, I wouldn't have landed the contract I have today still; providing hotel groups with beautiful photographs."

David wiped the rogue tear from his cheek. "You see, Detective, Ella was more than just a girl. She breathed life into us when we were dying inside. She showed us what it meant to be loved by someone for who we were and not because of the money in our bank account. Being in her presence alone brought us happiness no one else could fathom." He wiped another tear. "Sorry, it still breaks my heart that you haven't found the person responsible for tearing her apart and away from us. I'm amazed they didn't fire that police officer back then. He was utterly useless at his job."

"Did you know Officer Aldridge?" None of the others had even known his name, yet David seemed to know more. He was the break we were looking for.

"Did I know him?" He harrumphed. "He was a waste of space. Ella turned him down. Did you know that? His soul was black as tar. He filled his words with venom, and his actions were vindictive. Start there and I'm sure you'll find a heap of crap that could tarnish the police force. You're a detective, and if I had to guess, from out of town. Now, why do you think your captain brought you in?"

His words made me think carefully about who Eugene Aldridge was and his connection to our captain. "Thank you, David," I said. "Can I have your contact details in case I have more questions?"

"Sure, Detective," he said, handing me his business card. "I'm hardly at the studio, so call me if you need me."

"Thanks," I said, placing the card inside my notebook. "Let me know if you can't find Daniel and we'll create a missing person's case for him."

"Thanks," he said, pushing away from the wall. "There's no point staying here if he isn't here. Let me try his home."

"I'm heading that way," I said. "Mind if I follow you?"

"Sure."

Chapter Twenty-Four

HERE'S LOOKING AT YOU

Detective Steve Campbell

Mrs. Daniel Hanson opened the door, tucking blonde hair behind her ear. She wore tight fitting clothing, revealing a toned body. She stared deadpan at me, then at my I.D. then at Officer Graham's. Her green eyes reminded me of snake eyes. "What do you want, Detective?" she asked. Her tone harsh, like we had inconvenienced her.

"Mrs. Hanson—"

"Stephanie," she said, "my name is Stephanie. I have my identity, and I don't fall under my husband's inferior shadow."

I swallowed my words. My mouth dropped open slightly, but I quickly schooled my features. "Stephanie, do you know where Daniel is?"

"He's gone off to his hideaway cabin for a while. He's been stressing about something, and I'm assuming it's your fault, and that's why you're here."

Officer Graham shifted uncomfortably behind me. I ignored him.

"Would you mind giving me the address?"

"Of course I mind, but you asked so nicely." Her words dripped with sarcasm. She tsk'd and closed the door.

"What a bitch," Officer Graham said under his breath.

I agreed with him but didn't say it out loud for fear she'd open the door the moment I said it.

The door opened again, and she handed me a piece of paper. She was about to slam the door shut when I pushed it open again. "Before you go," I said quickly, opening the door wider. "Do you know Ella Turner?"

"What? All this fuss is about that slut. I thought she died."

"Yes, someone murdered her and we're trying to solve her case." Heat crept up my neck. "I take it you didn't like her very much?"

"None of us did. It's only weak men who became besotted over her. I don't know why. She was tacky, slutty, and useless. The woman couldn't get a job, and used these men for money. She came across as this girl in constant need of rescuing, and the men couldn't help themselves. They practically fell over each other trying to rescue her. It made them feel powerful and wanted. When in real life they were just as useless as she was."

I fisted my hands and sighed a frustrated breath. "Do you know who may have hurt her?"

"Anyone really," Stephanie said, tightening her jersey. She glanced to the side as if something more interesting was on the trees behind us. "I can't think of a specific person," she shrugged, "nah. Sorry fellows. I would say I hope you catch the person, but I don't care."

Before I could ask another question, she slammed the

door in my face. It took every muscle in my body to not slam my fists on the door and arrest her spiteful ass.

"What a bitch," Officer Graham said as we headed back to our cars. "No wonder Daniel wanted to be with someone else. That woman is terrible."

"I would like to ask her more questions though," I said, opening my car door. "I think drop your car at the station, it's on our way to Daniel's cabin, then we go through in my car."

Before I could close my door, David approached. "She's a piece of work."

I climbed out of the car again, nodding. "Yeah."

"Where did she say Daniel is?"

"He's gone to his cabin." I reached for the piece of paper, and he held up his hand.

"I know where it is. Are you going there now?"

"Yes."

"Okay, tell him I'll see him tomorrow. I have a meeting later this afternoon I can't miss it."

I followed the winding road toward Daniel's little hideaway cabin, making me envious. I couldn't wait for my weekend away with Alice as I was sure our cabin in the woods would be similar, only better; we wouldn't be answering questions relating to a murder.

"Wow," Officer Graham said as we drove up the driveway. "He must have money."

"Well, he inherited The Lounge from his grandfather and, most likely half of the money."

"I wonder if David got anything?"

"Not sure. We can ask him about his brother."

We found Daniel chopping wood on the far side of his cabin. When he heard our shoes crunching leaves, he spun around with his axe ready to strike.

"We come in peace," I said, holding up my hands.

"You startled me," he said, lowering the weapon. "What are you doing here? I answered all your questions."

"You forgot to mention details about your brother David, your awful wife, and that you may have been the last person to see Ella."

He tightened his hold on the axe, his nostrils flaring, but he had to have been counting to ten because he dropped the axe and wiped his forehead with his sleeve. A cool breeze blew from the water, making me shiver.

"Come on," Daniel said, walking past us. "Let me make you some coffee. I need a break anyway."

We followed Daniel inside his double story cabin that had magnificent views from the deck; the river in front and nothing but trees and nature surrounding him. I couldn't wait for my weekend away with Alice.

The cabin had luxurious furniture, a glass chandelier in the open plan living area and kitchen, with at least five bedrooms upstairs. We sat at the counter while he washed his hands, and then made us coffee.

I bit into the biscotti and sipped my coffee, a warm distraction from the cold outside and the discussion we were about to have inside.

"I met Ella the day she arrived in Ketchum. Jessica, who was my girlfriend then, was crying because I'd just broken up with her when Ella entered, asking for a job. I had no vacancies at that moment, but suggested she speak with David. He gave her a job but paid her little and misman-aged his finances. His company went broke, he sold it to Stanley, and then he turned back to his first love, photography. He took pictures of her and sent it to clients of mine, and he landed a sweet deal. I have the first picture he took of her in my office."

"I saw it. It's sensual and tasteful."

"Thanks," he said, and smiling for the first time. "Stephanie and I have an open marriage, just as long as I tell her everything and she gives me the 'ok'. She liked Ella at first, but then as time went on, I developed feelings for her, which is a big 'no' in Stephanie's eyes." He exhaled and rubbed his tired face. "It was wrong of me to fall for Ella, but I couldn't help it. It's not exactly something I could stop."

"Do you think your wife killed Ella?" Officer Graham asked.

David had mentioned that she had beaten Daniel. I was curious to know if he would say anything about it.

"Like I've said before, no. I love my wife, but she isn't the nicest person to live with, and she has a temper. I can never divorce her, and she uses that against me every moment she can."

"Why can't you divorce her?"

He sighed frustratingly and rubbed his face. "It's her money. Her cabin. Her house. Her money that financed The Lounge when I first took over. It turns a profit now, but I still owe her the money. And if I divorce her, I'm left with nothing because she'll take The Lounge away from me."

I felt bad for the guy, but unfortunately this happened often; people were stuck in bad relationships.

"Does she hit you?"

Officer Graham shot me a curious glance.

"Was it David?"

"Yes, he mentioned something like that," I said.

He sighed and sat down. "She never used to be like that,

but as the years went on, she became angrier and bitter, and violent."

"Do you think it's because of your lifestyle?"

"No, Stephanie has had many men over the years, so I don't think it's that. She's just... troubled, you know. She and her siblings had a rough childhood, and then there's all that money that changes people. Makes them entitled; mean. Anyway, Stephanie took her hatred of Ella out on me, and it stopped when she found out Ella was dead."

I felt sorry for Daniel. Here's this larger-than-life man who owned The Lounge, then came home where there was nothing but control and abuse. Nobody should suffer that.

"Was Ella ever afraid of you?"

He shook his head in disappointment. "She was jumpy that last week. Every time I touched her, she flinched like I'd hurt her. I never hit her, Detective. Ever. Something did happen though and when I asked her about it, she brushed it off. So, it wasn't me she was afraid of, but she was afraid of someone."

"You mentioned a Jessica earlier," I said, changing the subject. Daniel seemed uncomfortable sharing his personal life, but we had to ask the difficult questions. "Is this the same Jessica who Ella shared an apartment with?"

"Yeah." He glanced away.

"Was Jessica angry you chose the new girl over her?"

"I had already ended things with Jessica before Ella arrived. It wasn't her fault."

"Would Jessica hurt Ella?" Officer Graham said.

"No, I don't think so. No, she wouldn't have." He didn't seem convinced, and neither were we.

"Did you see Ella that night?" I asked, changing the subject again. Whether Jessica or Stephanie could hurt Ella, we didn't know and would have to question them again.

"I saw her," he said sadly. "She was saying goodbye to Kevin as I walked past. We had a drink. I kissed her on the cheek and planned for the next day. Why would I kill her if I made arrangements? I even kept the receipt." He opened a drawer in the kitchen and handed me the receipt for a pottery class and a 3-course dinner. "It was something she always wanted to do."

"Mind if I take this?"

"Yeah, sure, I've already taken pictures of it as a memento."

Officer Graham always had evidence bags with him and handed me one. "Thanks," I said, placing the item inside and giving it to him. "Why have you come out here? Your staff don't know where you are."

He rubbed his face. "I needed to get away. No offense, but the moment you guys started asking questions, all those memories of her surfaced and I'm just trying to move past them." He blinked back tears. "I loved her, and it devastated me when I saw her displayed in the field like garbage."

Perhaps the person responsible for killing Ella placed her there on purpose, to taunt Daniel. To show him what they were capable of doing and to remind him of his place. We needed to find evidence confirming that either Stephanie or Jessica was responsible.

Chapter Twenty-Five

LONG DAY

Detective Steve Campbell

The day was long, and I was tired, but I had to wait. "Do you see it?" I said, pointing at the screen.

Officer Graham leaned forward to see the person on screen and frowned. "See what?"

"The strange gait, Officer Graham. You and this person walk the same. I've seen you run, and that's what you look like." I played the video again. "There, do you see it?"

Officer Graham shrugged. "I don't know what you're talking about, Detective."

I hated that it came to this. I didn't want to run to Captain, but it looked like I had to sooner than expected. "Fine, be like that. I'm sure Captain would see it my way. Get ready to pack your bags." I grabbed my laptop and stuffed it inside the bag and slung it over my shoulder. I was almost out of my office when he reached for me.

"Wait!" he shouted and everyone in the open plan office glanced at us. I gave them a thumbs up. "Please, Detective.

Okay, fine, it is me. And believe me when I say I fucked up, I fucked up," he said with a loud sigh and sat down in my visitor's chair.

I spun around and placed my bag on the floor near my desk. "What happened?"

For the next forty minutes, Officer Graham explained everything; from his father getting caught up in drugs to killing himself, to his wife losing her job, to their child sick with leukemia and in remission. They had needed the money, and the amount he received from Jack paid for everything.

"Few knew about Stacey getting sick," he said. And I didn't want to be inundated with well wishes when all I wanted to do was get through the day. I'd never been so stressed before in my life, and then Macey lost her job. I couldn't cope anymore."

I understood what he meant. When Alice suffered her second miscarriage, I wanted nobody to know. The pats on the shoulder, the pity glances, the sideways hugs. I'd had enough of it all. Everybody meant well and tried to show their support, but sometimes one just wanted to go through the emotions alone.

I sat beside him in the second visitor's chair and listened intently. "I want to trust you, Officer Graham, I really do. How do I know you won't do something stupid like this again?"

"Please, Detective, please believe me. I understand why you can't right now, but I'm asking for forgiveness. I'm asking for a chance. If I lose my job, my pension, it will destroy my family. Where do I go? What do I do? Please trust me."

I opened my mouth to say something when he raised his hand, shushing me.

"I know. I should've thought of that before doing the dumb deed, and I regretted it the moment I took his money. All I ask is redemption. Trust that I'm an excellent officer and that I put my job first. I need to make amends. Please don't tarnish my reputation."

I leaned back in the chair and rubbed the bridge of my nose. "Okay, you're going to sign a confession about what you did."

"Done."

"Then I'm going to keep that statement in a safe place. If you mess up again, it's going to Captain along with the new offense."

"Deal," he said, with tears in his eyes. "Thank you, Detective. I won't let you down."

"This isn't for me, it's for you and your family. You mustn't let them down."

I sat on the porch swing waiting for Alice to return with our glasses. The sun had just set while the moon rose on the other side. A cool breeze moved the tree branches hypnotically.

I read the latest headline in the local newspaper, the third one this week, and shook my head. Someone was leaking information to the press. This looked bad for Captain, and us. There were things we didn't want the public finding out. My thoughts first went to Officer Graham but shook the feeling away, not after our earlier conversation. It wasn't him. It was someone else.

"You, okay?" Alice asked, holding my glass near my face.

I smiled up at her and took my glass. "Yeah, all good."

"You've been quiet all evening." She sat beside me, pulling the blanket over her legs. It hadn't snowed all day but there was a chill in the air.

"Just been thinking," I said, enjoying a sip, then placed my glass on the table in front of us.

"What about?"

Death. What happened to us when we left our loved ones? I thought about all the things I wanted to say. All the things I still wanted to do. Life had this sneaky way of catching up to us when we weren't looking, then smacking us in the face with the end. What happened to our souls? Did we go to a heaven or were we reincarnated? I had all these questions and because we weren't religious, there was no church I could go to for answers; but I doubted they would have the answers I needed, anyway.

I turned to look at the love of my life and I knew then that it would devastate me if she had to die before me. It would leave a scar so deep in my heart I didn't think I could recover.

I wrapped my arm around her shoulder and brought her closer to me. "What am I thinking?" I said. "About you and me, and this world, and that we need to take time out for each other. You know… that I mustn't work such long hours and to always be home for dinner." I kissed her forehead, then the tip of her nose.

She set her glass beside mine, placed her arm over my stomach, and rested her head on my shoulder. "I agree, and I love you."

"I love you more."

Chapter Twenty-Six

RELIEVED

Officer Graham

To say I was relieved that Detective Campbell wouldn't tell on me was an understatement. I fucked up and would prove to him he could trust me. My life was on track, Stacey was in remission, and Macey had a good job. Everything was fine. We had cases to work on and I was pulling my weight. I still struggled when we received feedback from Dr. Brink once she completed an autopsy, but I knew it would get better the more I attended.

I entered Detective Campbell's office, but he wasn't in yet. I placed his coffee on his table and headed for my desk. There were others in early and already busy with work.

I typed in Stephanie Hanson's name in our system and her mugshot flashed in front of me. I whistled. We arrested her for assaulting Daniel, but it was David who laid the charges. Daniel was still in hospital with wires keeping his jaw in place. And before she was married, she assaulted another woman who flirted with her then boyfriend.

Would Daniel have married her if he knew she was this violent?

Unfortunately, nothing stuck because they settled out of court. According to the articles I found online, Stephanie's father came to the rescue each time.

I dug further into Daniel and David; their grandfather left Daniel The Lodge, which had been struggling financially for a while. Then, after he married Stephanie, things turned around. They moved into a large home. They had property everywhere. And based on the various records I found, he refurbished The Lounge shortly thereafter, attracting a higher earning clientele, and things had been going well ever since.

Money made people do crazy things. That's probably the reason he still married her after she put him in hospital.

I couldn't understand why The Lodge wasn't given to both David and Daniel.

When we met Stephanie yesterday, I looked her in the eyes, which meant she was as tall as me, five foot seven. She had a license for a gun, not Daniel. Which I found interesting. It was usually the male who had the gun.

Something knocked on a chair, and I glanced up to see Detective Campbell enter his office.

"Morning," I said, leaning against the doorjamb.

"Oh, hey there," he said, placing his lunch on his desk. "What's up?"

I told him what I found about Stephanie and Daniel.

"Okay, no wonder I feared her," he said with a chuckle. "I don't know if it's her, though."

"How come? There's a good chance it's her."

"True, but the killer cut Ella neatly in half using the right tools. Stephanie seems to be all muscle and fists. I don't know if she has the mental capacity to be as elegant as our killer."

I stared at Detective Campbell for a moment too long. He may be right. "I see your perspective," I said, nodding. "Should we still interview her again?"

"Oh definitely, and Charlie's wife. The things David had said are enough for me to bring them in for a little chat."

"Should I start the process?"

"Please," he said, reaching for his coffee. "And thanks for this."

"No problem," I said, smiling.

Chapter Twenty-Seven

WAITING FOR DANIEL

Ella

I sat at our favorite table in the back of the restaurant at The Lodge. Daniel had to finish something quickly and told me to order a daiquiri, my favorite, which I did and now it was giving me brain freeze. Brian had added too much crushed ice.

"Everything okay?" Brian asked.

"All good, thanks, Brian. Can you check with Daniel again, please?"

"He said ten more minutes."

"Please check."

He smiled kindly. "Yes, Ma'am. I'll be right back."

"Thank you." Daniel and I hadn't been on many dates, and I felt vulnerable waiting alone for him.

I sipped quietly, watching couples enter the restaurant. When a tall, blonde woman made a beeline directly for me, a coldness spread throughout my body. I had only inter-acted with Stephanie twice before and she was never nice.

"Slut," she said when she stopped near my table. "Has Daniel finally stood you up?" She smiled slyly.

"No," I said softly. "He'll be here soon." I glanced nervously at Brian who was on the phone.

"I'm sure," she chortled, then leaned on the table. Her muscular arms were bare, her low top revealing, and the muscles along her jaw ticked. "I don't know what he sees in someone like you?" Her gaze was penetrating. "I'm not worried, because he'll get bored with you the way he always does. Toss you aside like the trash you really are."

Every time Daniel and I were together he made promises to see me often; which he kept. He had said he loved spending time with me, and always felt good when I was with him. Whatever Stephanie was talking about made little sense, but I knew not to respond when anyone was this hostile.

"He hasn't gotten bored with me because I'm actually a nice person. So, if he's ignoring you…" I left my sentence hanging and shrugged. She knew what I was getting at. As much as I hated playing her game, I couldn't help myself this time.

"You little bitch," she said, slamming her fist on the table, almost toppling my daiquiri.

"Maybe the only reason he stays with you is because you hold the divorce card over his head and threaten to take The Lounge away from him." I knew it was wrong to say that, but I had to. Mama always told me to stand up for myself.

Her face reddened, and she fisted her hands. She was about to pull the table away when arms grabbed her from behind, spinning her around.

"What the fuck are you doing, Stephanie?" Daniel said, seething with anger. "We had an arrangement."

"Ya, well, I want to change it."

"No," Daniel said, raising his chin.

"I don't care what you want, Daniel. I forbid you from seeing this girl ever again."

Daniel stared at her with murderous intent. He wasn't about to back down. "I don't care about the money, Stephanie. Take it all. You've been threatening me with divorce since I asked for that loan, and I've regretted it since. You've had many men in your bed, while I said nothing. Ella is the second girl I've had, and you're pulling this jealous crap on me. Go fuck yourself and get the fuck out of my lodge. You are no longer welcome here."

Daniel grabbed Stephanie hard by her arm and marched her out. He called security over, telling them she may never enter The Lodge again. As they reached the exit, he shoved her out and she almost fell.

I stood up and wanted to go to him when he returned, gesturing for me to sit. He smiled and sat across from me. He neatened his hair and straightened his tie and jacket.

"I'm sorry about that," he said, reaching for my hand across the table. "I hope you don't mind if I become poor?" He chuckled.

"Daniel, you know I don't care about that. Yes, I love to be spoiled, but your mental and physical wellbeing comes first. If that's what you want to do, I support you one hundred percent." I beamed at him.

"Thank you, my love," he said, kissing the top of my hand. "I needed to hear that."

We enjoyed the rest of our evening with champagne, food, dessert, and ended it in a room at The Lodge. It was the best evening I had ever had with Daniel.

While we were sleeping, I felt a strange sensation across my hand; like a feather caressing my skin. I opened my eyes just a smidge to see what he was doing, and he was drawing hearts on my hand with his finger; over and over, a heart. I didn't want to open my eyes completely and ruin the moment, so we lay there in silence. Daniel drawing his love for me on my skin, while I watched, and my heart swelled that much more for a man I could never fully have.

Chapter Twenty-Eight

INTERVIEWS

Detective Steve Campbell

Stephanie arrived at the police station with her lawyer. I escorted them to the interview room and sat across from her.

Stephanie wore a gray suit with a white floral blouse. Her blonde hair pulled tight in a bun, with thick, dark makeup, making her look scarier than the first time I'd seen her. Her green eyes seemed even more snake-like than ever.

Her lawyer, Frank, wore an equally boring gray suit, white shirt, and a green tie. He opened his briefcase on the table and handed me a stapled document. "This should be sufficient, Detective."

I read the document; a signed statement from Stephanie recalling where she was the day and night of Ella's murder. Also attached to the statement were photos with date and time stamps.

"You're very organized, Stephanie," I said, breaking the chilly silence.

"So?" she grumbled, folding her arms.

"Maybe you organized her death and needed the alibi?" I waved her statement.

She rolled her eyes. "So lame," she said, leaning forward. "I hated that girl, and I hated Daniel for bringing her into our lives. I wanted her gone, Detective, not dead. Daniel has worked himself to death since her murder and I hardly see him. It didn't improve my life, it made it worse. I can do nothing with Daniel now. He's a big, fat nothing."

She leaned over and whispered something into her lawyer's ear.

"Did you find him?" she asked.

"Yes, he was at the cabin."

"Good, because he hasn't been returning my texts or calls. I thought he might have finally killed himself." She laughed.

"When is he scheduled to be back home?"

"Today, but he hasn't as yet."

"Should we send someone?"

"No, it should be okay. Maybe he's extended his stay." She sounded bored.

"His brother David was looking for him."

"I saw him speaking with you on my lawn. He and Daniel haven't spoken in years." She thought for a moment. "Five, come to think of it. After that girl's death, David disappeared. Maybe those two had an argument."

"Why do you say that?"

"They're twins, Detective, they're always bickering. One jealous over the other. It's annoying if you ask me."

"Do you ever have a kind thing to say about your husband?"

"Haha, no, never."

"Do you beat your husband?"

She leaned over and whispered something into her lawyer's ear. "She doesn't have to answer that, Detective," the lawyer said. "We're done here unless you have reason to arrest my client."

Stephanie grinned the entire time her lawyer spoke.

It relieved me that the woman left with her lawyer. I'd sent a patrol car to check in on Daniel and was yet to receive feedback.

"Diane is here," Officer Graham said. "She's worse than Stephanie." His eyes widened.

"That's hard to believe, but I'll take your word for it." I shook my head. These women were something else.

"It's like they both came from the same bitter place. Yikes, mean women." Officer Graham opened the door to the interview room.

Diane wore body-hugging black pants and top, making it look like a second skin. She wore no underwear and stood in ball-crunching heels. She was applying red lipstick near the two-way mirror. Her dark eyeliner made her face seem harsher than it should be. There was nothing delicate about this woman, either.

Diane stared down her nose at me, threw her lipstick in her black leather handbag, and sat down. I wondered if she had a whip and a pair of handcuffs in her bag. The last case we worked certainly left an impression on me, making it easy to spot who lived that kind of lifestyle.

"Hi Diane, I'm Detective Steve Campbell, and you've met Officer Graham. Thank you for meeting with us today."

"It's not like you gave me a choice," she said. Her anger evident.

"How is your relationship with Charles?"

"Peachy," she snapped, folding her arms across her chest.

"No fights, altercations, nothing of the sort?"

"We're like any other couple who have been married for years, Detective. We fight, we get over it, we make up, we love each other again. It's the vicious cycle of life."

"What do you think of the girlfriends he brings home?"

"Well, for one, it amazes me any girl finds him attractive. I mean, have you seen his belly, his balding, his sweaty palms." She laughed. "The man is disgusting."

"What did you think of Ella Turner?"

"Slut, whore, gold digger."

"Why do you say that?" I continued asking my questions with respect, but I was coming close to losing my cool with her.

"She was the only girl who had so many men in her life. These poor losers did everything for this girl. It was pathetic."

"Did you hate her enough to kill her?" I wanted her gone, so I skipped the other questions and went straight to this one. Her berating her husband and the other men didn't sit well with me. Now I understood why they had said those things about her.

"No, Detective. I wish I had the honors, but whoever the person is, they beat me to it." Her grin stretched her face, and I imagined Diane enjoying inflicting pain on others.

"Did you ever hurt Ella?"

For the first time since the interview started, Diane had no quick retort. She hurt Ella.

"What did Ella do that you hurt her? And how did you hurt her?"

"I don't have to answer any of this." She shifted uncomfortably in her chair. "You know nothing."

"Well, tell me." We needed to bring Charlie in to hear what happened.

"I need a lawyer."

"We're just talking, Mrs. Roberts. There's no need for a lawyer unless you killed Ella. If you say you didn't kill her, then there's no need for a lawyer."

She pursed her lips. "Okay, fine, this girl comes into my Charles' life and turns everything upside down. He had never been so smitten with any other submissive coming into our home. But this girl, she bamboozled him, tricked him, made him her bitch."

As opposed to you, I wanted to say but kept quiet. I didn't want to anger Diane any more than she already was.

"I asked Charles to bring her home one evening so that I could play with her, teach her a lesson, and I might have gotten carried away with the strap-on dildo. I may have hurt her." She shrugged nonchalantly. "There was some blood, but she could still walk, so I didn't think I was that rough."

I felt Officer Graham's anger without having to look at him. I couldn't imagine what that girl had gone through, considering her small genitalia. Her autopsy report stated they had raped her anally, but there was no semen. Could the person have done the same to her when they killed her, like Diane had hurt her?

"You talk about your husband having a submissive," Officer Graham started. "Are you one?"

"Haha, gods no, I'm a Domme and Charles is MY

submissive. That man will eat my juices off my feet if I tell him to. He's my pet and I do with him as I please."

―――――――――

"I'm so glad that's over," I said, rubbing my face. "I feel like I need a shower."

"Me too," Officer Graham said, airing out his sweat stained uniform. "I can't believe that woman."

"Which one?"

"Both actually."

"Yeah, I know." I added extra sugar when I felt faint. Adrenaline had coursed through my veins listening to the two women, how they berated their husbands, spoke unkindly about Ella, and both wished her gone, dead, whatever.

"When I phoned Charles, he told me what Diane did to Ella," Officer Graham said. "He started crying, wished he could've stopped her, but he feared Diane. He had received similar treatment from her a week after Ella died because she wanted him to forget about Ella and move on with his life."

"Jesus," I said, taking a long, sweet sip.

"He couldn't walk for two days and thinks she permanently damaged some of the nerve endings back there." He gestured near his ass. "Said he needs to wear an adult diaper sometimes, and he's seeing a specialist to have that corrected."

"Does he want to press charges?"

"Too scared. She, too, holds the purse strings and all the control. She's a piece of work."

"If we can find others who Diane hurt to come forward, maybe they can all press charges together."

"Good idea. We could ask around the kink scene. Maybe Violet could help us."

"Excellent suggestion, Officer Graham. I'll phone Violet now."

To take my mind off the things Diane had done, the masochist, I phoned Violet to hear if she knew her.

"I know Diane Roberts," Violet said. She didn't sound enthusiastic. "I've banned her from my dungeon."

"Why?" I asked, playing with the pen on my table.

"The last time she left blood everywhere and her plaything had to be hospitalized."

"Can I ask you for their details?"

"Detective," she whined. "I don't like this. It's an infringement of their privacy."

"I'm sorry, Violet, but I need to know if this woman is our killer."

Chapter Twenty-Nine

DIANE'S PET

Detective Steve Campbell

Regina welcomed us into her home and offered coffee. She wore braids in her hair, and clothing that would make any hippy happy.

"I hope you don't mind," she said, pinching a 'cigarette' between her lips. "But talking about this makes me anxious and I need to relax."

"Go ahead," I said, not caring. She could have a line of cocaine if it helped our case.

She poured coffee into mugs for us, lit her spliff, and enjoyed a long drag. She held it in for ten seconds and exhaled. The smell of cannabis wafted in the air, and I tried in vain to wave it away. Hopefully, Captain won't smell it on us when we got back to the station.

"Diane, or rather Domme Vixen, found me online, and we got chatting," Regina said deep in thought. "After about a month, I agreed to meet up with her for a playdate at Violet's Play Spot & Anonymous Dungeon. At first, Diane was nice, kind, even gentle. But the moment she transformed into her *'Domme'*," Regina used air quotes, "her state of mind flipped a switch, and she went bat crazy on my body."

Regina had another long puff before continuing. Her hands shaking.

"I was bound so tightly on my wrists," she touched her scarred wrist, "and ankles my hands and feet turned purple, and when Diane bound my neck and started raping me anally, I screamed for help. I was bleeding everywhere by the time Violet entered with her security. Diane retaliated with a switchblade, slicing one security guy, forcing Violet to use the taser on her. The bitch went rogue, Detective. She's mentally insane."

I asked Regina to write everything down and sign it and she agreed to lay charges against Diane. Violet provided us with proof of the assault; the video showing Diane doing the deed. There was no way she could get off completely free. I only hoped it would help Charles help our case and if he knew of anything else, that he, too, could come forward.

Regina's story shocked us to our core, and we rode home in silence. I thought about Ella, who had suffered something similar, and I couldn't help but feel bad for these women.

"It still baffles me how someone can flip like that," Officer Graham said the moment we entered the police station.

"I know, and I hope word gets out to others who suffered a similar assault by Diane."

"Me too, Detective, me too."

"We need to establish a timeline and where Diane was

the night of Ella's murder." We had a few suspects who hated Ella enough to hurt her, and unfortunately, they were all women. From the interviews we'd had with the men, they all seemed to care deeply for her, but the women in Ella's life... they all wanted her gone. "And bring Jessica in for questioning."

"She too has been lying to us every step of the way," Officer Graham said, nodding. "I'll do that now."

I phoned Violet again and asked her to let me know if others approach her about Diane. Then I dialed Charles' number to let him know about Regina and that we could expect more.

"Hello?" he said.

"Mr. Roberts, it's Detective Campbell—"

"I can't talk right now," he whispered and ended the call.

I made a note to phone him later if he didn't return my call. A knock on the door sounded, and it was Officer Crick.

"Hi, what's up?"

"Hi," Officer Crick said, fidgeting with a shiny new watch. "We just received a call from David Hanson saying he found his brother's body. And the unit you sent has arrived on the scene."

Chapter Thirty

SECRETS ALWAYS COME OUT

Detective Steve Campbell

James was taking photographs while Dr. Brink saw to the body. Officer Graham was taking David's statement, and a female officer was speaking with Stephanie, who had arrived shortly after us.

Daniel's office was a mess. Whoever killed him was looking for something or they wanted it to look that way. He hadn't slept in his bed, and his bathroom was clean. The kitchen counter had stale, half-chopped vegetables, and a boiled over pot that messed on the stove.

Daniel knew his attacker. There were two plates set.

"Was he expecting you?" I asked, approaching David and Officer Graham.

"Yes, Detective, but only today. He wanted to tell me something important and whoever did this was with him last night," David said, pointing at the plates.

"Did he mention who?"

"No."

"And I don't suppose you know what he wanted to tell you?"

"No, he said he needed to tell me in person." David fidgeted with his jacket. "I have a feeling it's to do with Ella's killer."

"That he knew who it was?"

David nodded.

That was interesting, but what I couldn't understand was why didn't he tell me when I was here?

"When you arrived, was there anything strange upon entering?" I asked, glancing at Daniel's body with a rope around his neck.

"No," David said, glancing at his brother and choking on a sob. "He was hanging from the beam, and I cut him down. I didn't know how long he'd been hanging, and all I could think about was saving him."

"And you cut his restraints free?"

"Yes, sir. They tied his hands behind his back."

"And there was nobody else here?" I asked, glancing at Stephanie, who hadn't shed a tear. She didn't seem disturbed by Daniel's body, either.

"No, sir. I saw no one after I searched the cabin. And when I found the typed note… I phoned the police. He isn't suicidal, Detective."

"Sorry for your loss," I said, squeezing his shoulder. "I don't think he was suicidal either and we'll let you know what we find."

"Thank you, Detective."

I crouched near Dr. Brink, who was about to place Daniel's body in the bag. "What do you think?" I whispered near her ear.

She glanced at me, her green eyes wide. "Definitely homicide, Detective. He struggled. In my experience, if someone wants to kill themselves, they don't tie their hands behind their backs, and they don't struggle like he did. He broke his thumb trying to free himself, and his one nail tore. And a typed note, anybody can do that."

"Yeah," I said with a sigh. "I know."

"I'll call when I'm done," she said, smiling sadly.

"Thanks, Doc." I stood and headed outside. "I'm sorry for your loss," I said to Stephanie, who just finished speaking with the female officer. "Can anyone vouch for your whereabouts last night?"

"I was home, Detective," she said, folding her arms. "And you saw me this morning. I didn't kill him."

"Anyone with you?"

She visibly sighed. "No, I was home alone watching a movie, ate dinner, spoke with Daniel on the phone around nine. He told me he was about to eat and then he ended the call. I made myself some tea, watched half of another movie, then went to bed after ten. I met with you early this morning, went home, had a nap. I woke up when David called me, letting me know Daniel was dead, and I rushed over. It's an hour's drive from my home and got here shortly after you did." She put her hands in her pockets and glanced at Daniel's body.

"Were you two in a good space?"

"We've been married for over twenty years, Detective. We were in as good a space as anyone married that long. When all this crap about Ella came to the surface again, it weirded Daniel out, and I didn't know what to do about it, so I left him alone. I didn't fully understand the gravity of his love for her until recently."

"Do you think he killed himself?"

"No," she said, shaking her head, "absolutely not. And leaving such a vague typed letter is not his style. He has a beautiful handwriting and loves showing it off. He would never type it out. Whoever did this knew little about Daniel."

I made notes in my book and thanked her.

Officer Graham finished interviewing David, who joined Stephanie on the bench near the pool. They huddled together in sympathy.

"It seems David is the only one who likes her," I said when Officer Graham joined me on the veranda.

"He told me they kept in contact, even though he never spoke with his brother. It was the only way he could find out how Daniel was doing."

"Do you know what they fought about?"

"They fought over Ella, and then David got a photography gig in Dubai he couldn't pass up. He says the years just ticked by and then when he got back into town, he had to see Daniel."

"To me, it doesn't look like it's Daniel's death that brought them together." David and Stephanie held hands and whispered to each other.

"Well, he looks like his brother. Maybe Stephanie finds comfort in that, if that's at all possible."

"She only spoke unkindly about Daniel, not David."

"What's your point?" Officer Graham asked. His frown deepening.

"Maybe they're an item and haven't shared that news yet."

"Hmm, it's possible. We could always ask, but they could lie. Time will tell."

"Yeah." I rubbed my face. "When is Jessica coming to

the station?" I asked, changing the subject. It didn't matter if David and Stephanie were an item. It would matter, however, if they killed Daniel just so they could be together. Why not divorce?

Officer Graham glanced at his watch. "Soon."

Chapter Thirty-One

LIES, LIES, LIES

Detective Steve Campbell

"Jessica," I said as a greeting.

Her lawyer opened his briefcase and pulled out a folder. "My client has nothing further to say."

"That's okay," I said, holding my hand up to shush him. "I'll do all the talking."

I opened the case file slowly, meticulously, and watched Jessica squirm in her seat.

"Ever since we started the investigation, you've lied to us, held back evidence, withheld information, and continued with your fraudulent behavior by cashing those checks. To help your case and the list of charges against you, I suggest you help us, because after your interview, we're arresting you for fraud, obstruction of justice, and maybe murder." I cocked my head to the side, mimicking thinking. "We'll see." I grinned.

"You can't do that!" Jessica yelled. "I didn't kill her." She glanced at her lawyer who shrugged.

"Then who did? You must know something, Jessica."

She leaned forward and whispered something into her lawyer's ear, and he nodded. "Yes, I hated Ella for stealing Daniel away from me." I opened my mouth to comment but closed it again when she continued speaking. "He broke up with me the night we met her, but if it wasn't for her, I know we would've gotten back together again. I'm not proud of my behavior, Detective, so don't judge me. I was angry, desperate, and I took it out on her. She was this sweet little bird who couldn't hurt a fly, and all these men tripped over themselves to be with her."

"And you couldn't have any of them," I interjected.

Jessica's mouth twisted in disgust. She folded her arms across her chest and leaned back in the seat. "She pranced around the apartment bragging about all the things she received, and I just wanted a slice of her heaven, you know," she said, gentler this time. "After her disappearance, I was in between jobs and needed the money, so I cashed her check. And then kept on doing it. When she didn't return, I sold her jewelry to make ends meet, and I took her newest clothing. That's all, I swear. I didn't kill her."

"Who wanted her dead?"

"The women, Detective. The wives, the mother, any of them. They all hated her. I was enjoying a drink at The Lounge when Stephanie yelled at Ella. I wanted to cry it was that hectic, but deep down, it made me feel good that Ella got what she deserved. Then I felt guilty. Everybody in the restaurant was looking at Ella. Stanley was there with his mother, who, from her facial expression, enjoyed the show, too. She never seemed like one who hated anybody, but that evening I got the feeling she wanted Ella out of her son's life."

I didn't get the impression when we spoke with Mrs.

Whitaker and made a note to speak with her again. "Anything else you can think of?"

Jessica sighed. "I didn't hurt her, Detective. I saw what her body looked like and it's sickening anyone could do that to another person. They had to have known a lot about cutting a person up. I mean..." she shuddered, unable to finish her sentence.

That made sense. It's what Dr. Brink had also said when she did the second autopsy. Two of the men had some kind of medical training, while one was a surgeon. But all the men had an alibi.

"Have you heard about Daniel?"

Jessica frowned. "No? What about Daniel? Did he say something different?"

"We found his body earlier today—"

"What?" Jessica said, shaking her head.

"We're treating his death as a homicide."

Tears welled in her eyes.

"Do you know who may have wanted him dead?"

A rogue tear escaped, forcing Jessica to reach for tissues out of her bag. "No, I can't believe it. Are you sure it's him?"

"Yes, Stephanie and David were there to identify him."

Jessica choked on a sob. She tried talking but no words came out. I gave her a couple of minutes before continuing with my questioning.

"Do you know who wanted Daniel dead?" I asked again.

"No," she said. "I can't believe it. We still spoke. Do you know that?" I shook my head, and Officer Graham made a note. "It was bland conversation, asked how the other was, sent jokes, that kind of thing. If I had to think of one person who would hurt Daniel; Stephanie comes to mind. She hated him. I don't know why she chose him. Daniel always wondered what she saw in him because she always complained about everything he did." She wiped her face dry. "I can't believe it."

It was obvious Daniel's death came as a shock to Jessica and I didn't think she had anything to do with it. Unless she was a great actor, which I doubted.

After the interview Officer Graham arrested Jessica for obstruction of justice and fraud. Her lawyer would get her out the latest tomorrow morning.

"I wonder who's paying for her lawyer?" Officer Graham said.

"Not sure. Anyone offer to post bail?"

"I'll check once the paperwork comes in."

I sat at my desk. "Are you done with the timeline of events so we can nail down possible suspects?"

"Yeah, kind of. I still need to add the wives and their whereabouts."

Before heading home, I stopped at Stanley's medical device offices. The door was unlocked, so I took my chances and headed upstairs.

"Who is there?"

"Mrs. Whitaker," I called loud enough for her to hear me, taking two steps at a time. "It's Detective Campbell."

"What are you doing here?" she said.

I reached the floor as she was packing her things.

"I was on my way home and wanted to stop by."

"Oh," she said. "Is something the matter?" With bony fingers, she slowly packed her knitting needles into a large bag. She placed her clean cup and saucer into the cupboard behind her and locked it. She reached for her car keys and stood, waiting for my answer.

"No, nothing is the matter. I just wanted to ask a question or two."

"Sure, shoot."

"What's your relationship with your son like?"

"Stanley? Oh, he's my dear boy, Detective. He's my only child. I love him dearly."

"And you don't mind who he dates?"

"Of course I mind. She must be decent, caring, and compassionate. I only want the best for him."

"Did you like Ella?"

"Who?"

"The girl I spoke to you about the first time we met."

"Oh yes, she wasn't the best kind of girl for him. But if one thought about it, she wasn't his to have. She belonged to many men, therefore I didn't see them as a couple."

"Did you hurt her, Mrs. Whitaker?"

"What? Me? No, Detective. I'm an old woman," she raised her shaking hands, "I can barely write with them."

"Would Stanley hurt her?"

"No, Detective. As much as I didn't like her, he enjoyed her company. She made him happy."

"Did he love her?"

Something flashed in her features I couldn't quite place.

"Doubtful," she said. "That girl was unlovable."

Whether Mrs. Whitaker was telling the truth, I wouldn't know until I either had a confession, evidence, or something else to help my case.

Chapter Thirty-Two

TAKES TWO TO TANGO

Ella

"What the hell, Jessica?" I screamed from my room. "You used the spare key to get into my room, didn't you?" I stormed her room, her door slamming into the wall. "Stay out!"

"What's your problem? I wasn't in your room." She rolled her eyes.

I flicked her half-smoked cigarette at her. It struck her chest and fell to the ground. "Yes. You. Were," I said, enunciating each word slowly. I had to get out of this apartment. Unfortunately, I couldn't afford one on my own yet. I needed more money or someone to help me.

Jessica averted her eyes, no doubt realizing her mistake, but when she looked at me again, the smile creeping up her face left a chill in my body.

"Poor Ella, the girl with nothing to her name. No family. No friends. Only other women's men to keep her company. Your mama must be proud."

Heat filled my veins, and I saw nothing but black. I lunged for Jessica. My fingers curling around her neck, and I squeezed. Her larger hands found my neck, pulling me closer. Her knee raised, striking my chest. I let go of her neck. My hands going to my aching breast. Her hands gripped my hair, and she yanked backwards. I fell on my bum, my coccyx burning. As she lifted her knee to strike me in the face, I raised my stronger right hand and punched her pelvic area, and as she doubled over, I kicked her face with my boot.

"Wait! Stop!" Jessica yelled, landing on her bum. She quickly pushed herself away from me, striking the wall with her head.

I stood up and neared. Jessica slowly raked her eyes up my body, her hands nursing her bloody nose.

"Please, Ella, truce." She whimpered in pain.

"You should've thought of that before attacking me, Jessica." I closed the distance. "This is the last time I'm warning you." As I walked past, I kneed her in the face. Her head hit the wall again, and she fell forward, unconscious. Before exiting, I pushed her over hard, ensuring she crashed to the floor with a loud thud. "Bitch."

I slammed my head into my doorframe until a green/blue bruise blossomed without breaking the skin. I dressed and applied some makeup; enough to hide the bruising, but not so much Daniel couldn't see what had happened.

I arrived at The Lounge, using the back exit near Daniel's office. I knocked twice on his office door, waiting patiently for his answer.

"Come in," he called.

Slowly, I opened the door and entered. I hid behind my hair. "Hi babe," I said sweetly. It was only when I reached him, did I show him my face and sad eyes.

"What happened?" He bolted out of his chair and closed the distance. His hands reached for my face as he scanned the bruises. "Who did this, Ella?" he said angrily.

I squeezed a tear out and glanced up at him. "Jessica came out of nowhere and attacked me. I did everything I could to get away from her."

Anger radiated off him. His hands bunched into fists. "You must get away from her," he said, trying desperately to hide his rage but failing. "Please let me move you to your own apartment."

"Would you do that for me?"

"Yes, of course." Daniel pulled me in for an embrace. "I want nothing bad happening to you."

"Okay," I said. My smile reaching my eyes. "Can we look for a place sometime soon?" I played with the short hairs near his neck.

"Sure," he said, holding me tightly.

I pressed my head against his chest and listened to his heartbeat; it was so calm, helping me relax. Daniel was the safest of the men in my life. Although it wasn't his money, he would do what he could to help me, even if it meant using The Lounge's resources which he owned. I couldn't turn to Charlie because Diane scared me, and I didn't think he could stand up to her when it counted. Stanley lived with his mother, which creeped me out. He always asked her for permission to do anything. No matter what I tried, I couldn't get him off her breasts. David was gone; he'd left me when I needed him the most. The only one I could really count on was Daniel.

"Thank you for caring about me so much," I said into his chest, breathing in his scent.

"I love you, Ella," he said, kissing the top of my head. "If I could divorce Stephanie, I would do that tomorrow—"

"I know it's difficult for you. She would leave you with nothing. I'll take what you can offer."

I left his office feeling lighter and much happier. Next month this time, I'd be in my new place and far away from that vile Jessica. I passed the restaurant area, and something caught my eye. I looked in that direction and saw David. My heart skipped a beat, knowing he was back in town and wanted to surprise him with a kiss. As I neared, my steps slowed. A woman's hands combed his hair, and they turned around. Stephanie. She was here in Daniel's restaurant, flaunting her affection for my David.

She let him go. I was stuck between wanting to say hi or leaving them alone. David left a couple of months ago without saying goodbye, so seeing him now brought back memories. If I didn't greet him, it would forever haunt me.

I snuck behind him and covered his eyes. "Guess who?" I whispered near his ear.

His powerful hands gripped my wrists, and he chuckled. "Only tiny wrists such as these can belong to Ella."

"Yes," I said with a giggle. "It's me. When did you get back in town?" I playfully slapped his shoulder. "Why didn't you say goodbye before leaving?"

David turned around, still chuckling. "I couldn't find you, little one," he said, smiling when his eyes met mine. "And I got back today for your information. I came here first and bumped into Stephanie."

"Shouldn't you be somewhere else?" Stephanie said, reaching for David's hand, and pulling him away from me.

"Now, now, ladies. You don't have to fight over me," David said, smirking. "There's more than enough of me to go around without anyone feeling left out." He let us go.

"Hasn't Daniel banned you from being here?" I asked, glowering at Stephanie. "And does he know you want to fuck his brother?" My eyes darted to her hand reaching for David.

"You little—" Stephanie raised her hand to strike me when David caught her, pushing her away from me.

"Stop it!" he demanded. "I've had enough fighting. First me and Daniel, now you with Ella. Enough!" He let her go, and she almost stumbled. Patrons stared, with someone nearby gasping.

"At least there are witnesses this time." I was alluding to an altercation where she bumped me, and I fell into the pool. She ran away so quickly others thought I was drunk and had fallen in, embarrassing Daniel when he came to see what had happened.

Stephanie smiled sinisterly. "Next time, I'll hold your head underwater."

"Stephanie!" David chastised. "Enough."

There must've been something in David's expression I couldn't see, because Stephanie immediately recoiled. "Yes, David."

"Good. Now, girls, leave each other alone." He turned to me. "Go, Ella, and stay safe." He cupped my face and kissed me chastely. "I'll find you and we'll talk before I leave again. Maybe you can come with me and leave all this behind you."

"I miss you," I whispered against his cheek, blinking back tears. I reached for his hands on my face and kissed his palm. "Don't forget me."

He didn't find me before leaving, and I suspected it had something to do with Daniel. They fought; it was worse this time. Daniel shared how much he hated his brother, wished him dead. I assumed it's because David wanted to take me away from him too.

I thought about David until my last day.

Chapter Thirty-Three

MOTHER DEAREST

Ella

"I just need to fetch something from home," Stanley said, parking the car in his driveway.

I groaned inwardly. "Okay, my love. Do you need help with anything?" I offered, opening my car door.

"No," he said quickly. He stopped, stared at his house, then approached. "You know what, yes, come inside." It surprised me he changed his mind. Usually, he preferred me staying in the car even though I always offered to join him. "Mother won't mind," he said, exhaling a shaky breath. He opened my door wider and helped me out. He reached for my hand, guiding me to the front door. "Mother," he called out as we entered. He closed the door behind me, squeezing my hand tightly.

I followed him into the kitchen when footsteps down the stairs echoed in the house.

"Stanley? Is that you, boy?" Mrs. Whitaker entered the kitchen, but when she saw me, her smile dropped, turning her usual pleasant face into a bitter scowl. "Oh, you're with the whore again."

"Mother! Please stop calling her that."

"That's what she is, Stanley. She's been with at least three men since last week and she's manipulating all of you. I mean, look at her," she said, pointing at my dress. "She's nothing but a whore."

"That's enough," Stanley said, pushing me behind him. "Call her that one more time and you're moving to the retirement home tomorrow."

"How dare you, boy? I gave birth to you and raised you all by myself after your father passed away. I took care of you; you *will* take care of me."

"They can look after you there and you can make friends your age."

"I'm not old."

"You're old enough, Mother." Stanley grabbed the picnic basket, squeezed my hand again, pushing me slightly to the right-hand side toward the back door.

"If your father saw what you were doing with that girl, he would see the same as me."

"Father left you long before he died. You're smothering me, just like you smothered him. No wonder he couldn't stand you."

"Stanley Henry Whitaker. I didn't raise you a Christian boy so you could speak to me this way."

"I left Christianity long ago, Mother. You know this." Stanley's face reddened as he spoke. He had never mentioned religion to me, and now I understood why. His mother probably beat it into him as a young boy. "We're leaving. I want you packed and ready to leave by the time I come back. They've a space waiting for you."

"Stanley, please," she cried. "No, you can't do this to

your flesh and blood. I sacrificed everything for you. You owe me. And you need to look after me. I'm the only woman who can please you."

Ick. I didn't want to know what she meant by that, but Stanley didn't respond. He opened the back door, motioning for me to exit first.

"No!" His mother lunged for him. The picnic basket flew into my back. I tripped, falling down the stairs, crashing knees first. Stanley stumbled and crashed half on top of me, half off. He'd stuck his hands out, ensuring he didn't land with his full weight on me.

My body and right-side cheek slammed into the grass; my clothing soaked right through.

Stanley rolled onto the grass beside me and moaned.

"You'll leave when I give you permission to leave," Mother Awful said, traversing down the stairs like a living nightmare. I watched her stare at me; and I swore I felt her hate beat against me. "She needs to go, Stanley," she said with disdain. She filled her words with a hollow rage, making all the hairs on my body stand on end.

I moved, so that I saw her, while Stanley sat up right. "Stop, Mother," he said, but she didn't stop.

Mother Awful approached me with purpose. I moved backward on my bum. Her right hand was behind her back, and I could only imagine the weapon she held.

"Say goodbye, boy," she said and lunged for me.

But Stanley was quicker than the old goat and slammed his shoulder into her. The large knife went flying and landed blade first into the wet ground near my leg. I wet myself from fright. Mother Awful crashed to the ground with a loud thud, groaning.

Stanley stood between her and me, and he pointed. "Last warning, Mother. You may have brought me into this world, but I'll take great pleasure in taking you out of it."

———————

"How are you feeling?" Stanley asked.

"I'm okay," I said, smiling. "The sandwich you made was delicious." I ate the last piece.

"Would you like something else to eat? Maybe some fruit? More wine? Are you sure your body isn't sore?"

"I've had enough," I said, reaching for his hand. "I'm fine. Stop fussing over me."

"Are you sure?"

"Yes," I said, leaning over and kissing his left cheek. "I'm fine. Now don't worry. Let's not have your mother ruin the rest of our time together."

"You're right," he said, glancing at the ducks on the water.

"It's a beautiful day," I said, lifting my chin toward the sun. "So warm." My eyes closed.

"You're like a sunflower."

His soft lips found mine. Then his hands cupped my face, and I melted into him. I kissed him back with all the love I had to offer. I wanted him to feel loved and appreciated by me. I wanted him to forget about any past trauma, and to enjoy the present moment with me.

"I love the way you kiss me," he said. "It's like I can feel what you feel in that moment." He chuckled. "I sound like a girl, but you know what I mean."

I nodded. "I enjoy spending time with you."

"Do you feel the same way for the others?" He quickly glanced away.

I didn't feel like going into this but knew I had to answer

him at least once. "I care for each of you differently," I said, caressing his cheek so he would look at me. "I kiss each of you differently, too. My love for you doesn't become less because I'm with one of the others. And you should know by now, I have a lot of love to give." I grinned.

"I know, it's just—"

I pressed my index finger against his lips. "Kiss me, before our present moment is gone forever."

Chapter Thirty-Four

DAVID

Ella

"Move your arm up just a little and closer to your ear," David said, holding his camera near his face.

"Like this?" I asked, moving as he instructed.

"Perfect, now hold it." He snapped a few shots, moved closer to me, snapped a few more from different directions.

"I want to see what they look like," I said, shifting my body slightly and looked at him with hooded eyes.

"Don't look at me like that, Ella."

"Or what?"

"You know?"

"No, I don't," I teased.

David placed his camera on the other side of the couch and crept up my body, forcing me to slide down. He grabbed my wrists and held them above my head. He leaned forward and kissed me.

I snuggled into him, enjoying his warmth. "This feels nice." I felt safe with David; he had no jealous wife giving him grief, or a mother telling him what to do. It was just me and David. But... he had no roots here and couldn't support me the way I needed.

He hugged me tighter and kissed the top of my head. "When are you meeting Daniel again?"

I hated when he asked about his brother. The last time I told him where we'd be, he interrupted our date. "We haven't scheduled one yet," I lied. He pinched the skin near my ribs. "Ow," I cried, sitting up.

"Don't lie to me," he said, sitting up, and playing with an imaginary piece of string.

"I don't want to tell you because you cause trouble. Daniel hates it when you interrupt our dates. He doesn't interrupt yours."

He visibly sighed and scratched the stubble along his jaw. "I hate this, Ella. I don't know how the others can do this, knowing you're involved with other men." He climbed out of bed, glaring at me.

Tears welled in my eyes. When I blinked, I turned away.

"Dammit," he said, and pulled on underwear. "I don't want to fight. I understood what I was getting myself into, but things change. I just wish..." he left his words hanging.

"I know," I said, scooting off the bed and slipping on my underwear. "You'd love me more if I were available the way *you* want. You'd care more for me if it was just me."

"That isn't what I mean." He sighed.

I pulled on my jeans, then my top.

"Don't go," he said, closing the distance. "I'll make us some coffee. We can have something to eat." He pulled me in for a bear hug. "I don't want our date ending in anger.

Stay with me," he whispered the last part and kissed the top of my head.

I stared into his pleading green eyes, hoping he could see the sadness in mine. This was difficult for me. I enjoyed all their company. I could never pick one. It was possible for me to love all of them equally, yet differently.

"Let me help make," I said, smiling, but it didn't reach my eyes. I didn't want us to fight either and would rather enjoy our time together.

He cupped my face, and with his thumb, wiped tears off my cheek, and kissed the tip of my nose.

If I'd known this was the last time we'd be together, I would've stayed the night...

Chapter Thirty-Five

EVERYONE'S GUILTY

Detective Steve Campbell

I rubbed my face and pushed the mug of coffee away. If I had another cup of coffee, I'd throw up. I stood, then paced. Ella's timeline stared back at me.

"They're all guilty," Officer Graham said, sitting in the meeting room corner like a naughty kid.

"Yeah," I said, staring at the board, missing the crucial piece that could solve the puzzle. "Stephanie, Diane, and Mrs. Whitaker hated Ella. The men wanted her for themselves, and possibly jealous of each other. Ella saw all the men that week, except David. Kevin that day, and Daniel had a drink with her before she died. Then where did she go?"

"The clerk at the Roadside Inn spoke with Kevin but never saw Ella that evening at all. I think it happened as Kevin said; he gave her the key and went home."

"Was blood found in the room?"

"No."

"What about The Black Dahlia case?" I asked. Officer Graham had been studying the two cases. The problem with this is we were too close to the case to see the bigger picture; we were missing something.

"The motel owners admitted to finding one of their cabins covered in blood and fecal matter," he turned the page, "and it's believed they murdered her there. That's not what's happening in our case, though."

"Okay, fine. So, Ella says goodbye to Kevin," I repeated, pointing at the timeline, "has a drink with Daniel. The restaurant owners verified this and said Daniel left before Ella did. Nobody sees her going to the room. Someone finds her there, takes her to the forest where her black top snags on a branch. Then they take her to a place where they can torture her and cut her in half." A shudder ran through me. I hated sounding so clinically numb when someone mistreated another human, but I did it for my mental health; I had to put distance between me and the victim.

"Yeah," Officer Graham said, closing his book. "I wonder if Daniel sat in his car for a while and watched Ella go to her room, then witnessed someone kidnap her. Maybe that's what got him killed."

"But why now?" I asked, frowning.

"Maybe he only made the connection now and confronted that person. He wanted justice served and got himself killed."

I stared at Officer Graham. "You may be right. Now all we have to do is figure out who's lying."

Chapter Thirty-Six

DADDY DEAREST

Detective Steve Campbell

"Detective," Officer Crick said, knocking on my office door frame.

"Yeah," I said absentmindedly. The photos and autopsy report on my desk had all my attention. There had to be something we'd missed, and I was adamant about finding it.

"Mr. Turner is here to see you."

I whipped my head up, sending pain down my neck. "Where is he?" I asked, standing.

"The small meeting room, Detective. Officer Graham is making him tea."

"Thanks," I said, and passed him, but not before seeing something that looked like a new tattoo on his arm. It peaked out from under his sleeve. "I'm just glad he finally arrived."

Officer Graham gave Duncan his tea and sat down. He looked up when I entered the room, giving me a curt nod.

"Mr. Turner," I said, proffering a hand, "so glad you finally made it."

"Yeah," he said, shaking my hand limply. I wiped my hand dry on my pants and sat beside Officer Graham. "I would've gotten here sooner, but like I said when you called, I needed money first."

"I'm glad you're here."

He smiled, revealing stained and crooked teeth.

"I'd like to find out about Ella's arrest in 1993," I asked.

He shifted uncomfortably in his seat. "Um, yeah, she was with me that day and a friend of mine bought her a drink. Unfortunately, the cops raided and discovered she was underage. We were both arrested that day."

He needed to be rewarded for being the father of the year.

"What happened to Ella's mother?" Although I already knew, I wanted to hear his version of the story.

"It was an unfortunate event," he said, glancing at his dirty hands in his lap. "Nancy and I had one of our usual fights. She grabbed her car keys and drove off. They found her car in the river and her body washed ashore. It devastated Ella when I told her. She didn't speak to me for a week; blamed me for her mother's death. Then when the lawyer showed up telling me where the money was going—"

"That must've angered you."

"Of course," he said, the veins in his head bulging. "I was the husband and put up with her complaints our entire marriage. That money was meant to come to me. How dare she leave it all to a child?"

"But you took the money, anyway."

"Yeah, Ella shared with me. She ensured I had clothes and ate every day. Poor girl. She still looked after me."

"Did you keep in contact with Ella when she moved here?"

"Kind of," he said, fidgeting with his hands on the table, "she phoned me mostly."

"I take it your relationship was okay, then?"

"Yeah," he shrugged, "like any father and daughter relationship."

"You didn't find it strange that she hasn't contacted you in five years?" I didn't want to ask this over the phone when I first spoke with him because I wanted to see his face when he answered.

"Uh, well, yes, of course I found it strange."

"Just as long as you continued to receive half of the money," I said, with no emotion behind the words.

Duncan averted his eyes.

"The authorities took you into custody the day after her murder. Can you tell me what happened?"

He looked up. His expression was hard and emotionless. "I phoned to ask her for money. Whoever had answered told me she wasn't coming back, but I'd still get my money."

"Was it a male or female you spoke with?"

"Female."

Chapter Thirty-Seven

DANIEL

Detective Steve Campbell

After our interview with Duncan, we brought him to the morgue, where Dr. Brink showed him Ella's face for identification; hiding the lower half of her face. He nodded, and in silence, left the building. When I asked where he was staying, he didn't answer.

As heartless as I sounded, but I didn't care. Duncan may have had a hard life, but it seemed it was one he did to himself; an alcoholic father who only cared about his daughter when she sent him money. He had a problem now because that money would be stopped by the lawyers.

Dr. Brink pulled out the next gurney from the fridge and pulled back the sheet. Daniel Hanson laid peacefully on the cold tray. His body white as snow.

"His death was quick," Dr. Brink said, pointing at his neck. "They pushed him from the second floor. The force was so great it fractured the upper cervical spine at C2 and transecting the spinal cord."

"How do you know he didn't jump himself?" We had already discussed this at the scene but now I needed to make sure what his cause of death was so that I knew how to proceed. Was it a suicide or homicide?

"He tried to get out of the restraints that tied his hands behind his back," Dr. Brink said matter-of-factly. "If he was alone, he wouldn't have had the restraints in the first place. But the person responsible had tied his hands so tightly behind his back, and then kicked him from behind. I found a bruise on his back the outline of a boot." She lifted his shoulder and called me over.

"Jeez, that's quite a bruise," I said, staring at the large purple mark on his back.

Officer Graham came close enough to see and then went back to the chair that now remained in the corner for him.

"Size nine men's boot."

"Toxicology?"

"Alcohol and a barbiturate. They wanted him docile."

"Do you think he knew them?"

"Definitely. James found a half-washed plate, knife and fork in the kitchen sink, but left Daniel's crockery on the table. We found no DNA or prints unfortunately. They wiped the place down. Although," she said, headed for the back of the room and returned with a bag. "We found traces that didn't belong; pastel blue fibers from clothing."

I held the evidence bag with the blue fibers, then held it up for Officer Graham. "Do you remember anyone wearing a blue jersey, maybe?"

"Maybe," he said, frowning. "Will review my notebook."

Officer Graham sometimes wrote who wore what while interviewing them. Hopefully, he wrote that down.

"We found another smaller footprint outside, and trying

to figure out the type of shoe." Dr. Brink took the evidence bag from my hands and placed it in the tray again at the back of the room.

"Two people?" I asked.

"Seems that way, Detective. Unless he had a visitor prior to the killer."

I wondered if the smaller print belonged to one of the women. Jessica was shocked when we informed her about his death. Therefore, I doubt it was her. Stephanie seemed like she didn't care but had no alibi. We were yet to speak with Mrs. Whitaker and Diane.

"Thanks, Doc," I said, then glanced over my shoulder. "You ready?"

"Yeah," Officer Graham said, approaching. "Where to next?"

"Aldridge."

Chapter Thirty-Eight

OFFICER EUGENE ALDRIDGE

Detective Steve Campbell

"Show me again," I said, staring at Eugene Aldridge's tombstone.

"Here," Officer Graham said, handing me the note in an evidence bag that was left on my desk before we viewed Daniel's body.

'Meet me at Eugene Aldridge's grave at 2pm'

"Did anyone see them drop it off?" I asked, handing him back the note.

"Nobody saw anyone in your office."

"Do you think it's someone internal?"

He raised a shoulder. "We'll find out." He jerked his chin. I spun around to see who was approaching.

The case had taken us from one suspect to another, only to find that person might be innocent or that person could be guilty, but we had no evidence or witnesses. There were so many people involved in this that it amazed me we had even gotten this far in such a short time. Then there was Aldridge. He worked a homicide case he wasn't supposed to. Then he buried it. Why? I'd like to know how that was possible. What I didn't expect was to see Captain approach us.

"Captain?" I said, his presence here a question.

"Boys," he said, smiling. "I didn't want anyone seeing or hearing us talk about Aldridge at the station."

"Why?" I asked, squinting at him. Captain Payne had done nothing like this since I'd joined. Why the cloak and dagger? We could've met in his office.

"We have a mole," he said, standing beside me with his feet slightly apart and his hands on his hips. His bushy eyebrows crinkling together. "Someone is leaking information to the press, and I don't want this getting out. Yet."

I turned slightly, so the sun didn't stab me in the eyes.

Officer Graham had his notebook and pen ready.

"I was cleaning my office when I came across a second file for Aldridge. It was stuck right at the back of the metal drawer." He pulled a brown folder out from behind his back and handed it to me. "Before I became captain, Dennison was in charge." He pointed at the folder. "You'll read in here what he had to say about Aldridge." He shook his head. "Aldridge had targeted my aunt because he knew I was moving up the ranks and would be his boss one day. The amount of crap he used to pull; stealing evidence, paying prostitutes, involved in illegal activity. The list goes on and on."

"Why didn't Dennison do anything about it before he left?"

"He was busy with his case, then he died in a car accident. This file went right to the back of the drawer."

"If Aldridge knew he was under investigation, why didn't he destroy it?"

"After Dennison died, we locked his office. When I started, I couldn't find his file. Dennison's assistant didn't know where it was, so I asked her to create a second one. I had my suspicions, but I didn't know it was this bad." He pointed at the folder in my hands.

I opened the folder and skimmed through it. "Look at his known associates."

"The Whitaker's?" Officer Graham said, shocked.

Relief washed over me. We needed a break in the case, and this could be it.

"Why was he involved with them?" I asked.

"When I started out as a detective," Captain Payne said. "We investigated a surgeon who was botching surgeries. His wife came forward as a witness. She and Aldridge became extremely close, intimate even, and we all suspected the son was his and not the surgeons. The surgeon committed suicide before we could arrest him, and the case was closed. Aldridge would joke and say he thought the surgeon was The Black Dahlia killer because of how he botched the surgeries—"

"Can we see those files?" I asked.

"I've asked Daphne to get those for you. They're under a lot of dust, but you'll have them by tomorrow."

"Thanks Captain," I said, feeling hopeful. I glanced at Officer Graham. "We need to speak with Mrs. Whitaker after we've gone over those files."

Chapter Thirty-Nine

DINNER WITH GUESTS

Detective Steve Campbell

Olivia was already in the kitchen helping Alice when I arrived home. I knew she'd be here, but somehow, it still irked me. It seemed we had adopted Olivia and had her over regularly for dinner. I shouldn't complain; Olivia was good company for Alice. She helped Alice come out of her shell a little more and I would forever be grateful to her. But sometimes I wanted a quiet evening alone with my wife.

"Hey, honey," Alice said, waving at me. "Dinner is almost done." She wiped her hands on a dishtowel, opened the oven door and steam blew her hair back. She wiggled her eyebrows. "It's going to be delicious."

I smiled. I hadn't seen Alice this excited about food in a long time. "How are you?" I asked Olivia.

"Good," she said, sitting at the table and eating a carrot. "The shop is busier than ever, and things have been going okay since I got back."

"I'm glad to hear," I said, washing my hands. "How is Violet?"

"She's okay," Olivia said, but there was something in her tone that made me look at her.

"Sure?"

"Yeah, I mean, um, she's been a bit tired. She blames the stock taking and accounting that needs to be done, but…"

"But what?" I sat at the head of the table.

"I don't know. It could just be the stress of the ordeal we went through, but I sense there's something else. I tried talking to her today about it, but she brushed me off."

"Okay." I adjusted my knife and fork, so they were straight. "After this case, I'll check in on her." I rubbed my face.

"She'd like that," Olivia said, smiling. "You look tired."

"Yeah, this case is taking its time getting done."

"Enough shop talk, let's eat," Alice said, placing the dish with the roast lamb and potatoes in the center of the table. The delicious smell made me salivate.

I sat back and watched Alice and Olivia exchange pleasant words about the food and how their day went.

Alice dished food on my plate, giving me a look that told me she was in a good space. I reached for her elbow and squeezed gently, making her smile shyly.

In times like these, I loved coming home after a long day at the office working a tough case, and seeing Alice so happy told me things were going to be okay.

Chapter Forty

THE SURGEON'S CASE

Detective Steve Campbell

"Jeez," I said when I saw the thick folder waiting for me in my office. "That thing is massive." I picked it up, feeling the weight of the old investigation.

"Yeah," Officer Graham said, holding two coffees in his hands. "I waited for you to get in before attempting to look at it."

"Should we take this to the meeting room where there's more space?" As much as I loved working inside my office, it wasn't big enough for two people to move around comfortably. The meeting room next door was bigger and brighter, and for some strange reason, the air was better there; I seemed to stay awake.

"Sure, I'll grab my laptop, too."

Once we settled down and each had a stack of papers to read through, I picked up the first page; a witness statement dating back to 1957. It explained what had happened to her before, during, and after her surgery.

Mrs. Joanna McCall complained about her knee. Dr. Christopher Wilson advised her she needed a joint replacement and booked her in for the procedure. Two days later, she woke up with an amputated leg from mid-thigh. She had said Dr. Wilson was adamant she sign his medical liability forms before the operation.

Mr. Grant Thomas needed a hip replacement. He, unfortunately, died on the operating table. His wife, Mrs. Thomas, filed the complaint when she saw his corpse. The pictures showed how Dr. Wilson had cut his body not related to hip surgery.

Miss Elizabeth Hussain was in a car accident and Dr. Wilson was assigned to her operating table assisting another surgeon. The other surgeon laid a complaint against Dr. Wilson for negligence. Apparently, he sliced the wrong leg, almost amputating her from the knee down. The other surgeon kicked him out of the operating room and managed to save both legs.

"These are terrible," I said, rubbing my eyes. "I've read three cases now and can already feel the anger boil inside me. How could this guy get away with so much for so long?"

"I know," Officer Graham said, raising the statements he had read. "Four cases here. All botched operations where he maimed the patient, or they lost their life."

"I wonder whether Dr. Wilson enjoyed his taste for blood and then couldn't help himself."

"Are you referring to The Black Dahlia?"

"Yes," I said, arching an eyebrow. "What if it's him, and we just solved one of the most famous unsolved murders?"

"It could be." He shrugged. "The Black Dahlia was in 1947, and these cases happened ten years later." He raised his stack of papers. "It's like he disappeared to find a wife and appear normal, to blend in with society, but he couldn't stop thinking about his first kill and started butchering his patients."

"Was his medical license valid during that time?" I searched the stack of papers and found what I was looking for. "Nope, the medical board couldn't find him."

"Jeez, that's scary," Officer Graham said. "It makes me want to question each doctor I consult with."

"Yeah, me too." I touched the wooden table, grateful everyone we had met and consulted with was the real deal.

"We should show the FBI this," Officer Graham said, picking up another stack of papers.

"After we've solved our case."

"So where does Aldridge fit in."

"Here," I said, holding the statement by our very own captain. "A young Detective Payne investigated the case with Aldridge. There's a side comment where he states he thinks Aldridge may be involved with Delilah Wilson—"

"Delilah sounds like Dahlia. That's interesting."

"Maybe coincidental?" I shrugged. But I knew nothing about this case was coincidental. "And then the surgeon ends up hanging himself."

"Like Daniel."

"Yes, like Daniel."

"Is Mrs. Whitaker still Delilah?" Officer Graham said, then started typing on his laptop. "I can't find her."

"Maybe she's still Delilah Wilson," I said, reaching for the next stack of papers that included photos of the victims before and after their procedures. They were gruesome. Dr. Wilson must've enjoyed hurting them to continue the way he did. The only picture of him I could find he was standing beside Mrs. Joanna McCall. He was grinning, and that was after her ordeal. He was sick. Dr. Stanley Whitaker looked nothing like Dr. Wilson, but Eugene was another story.

"Yeah, it's still Delilah Wilson."

"What about Stanley Whitaker?" I asked. "Is that his real name, and is he a registered doctor?"

Engrossed with his laptop, Officer Graham tapped away on his keys and wrote notes. "You won't believe this," he started, "Eugene's mom's maiden name was Whitaker."

"Well, I'll be darned."

"She died a year after they discovered Dr. Wilson hanging in their garage."

"How did she die?"

"Car accident, and," Officer Graham continued typing, "Stanley is registered, but I can't find evidence of him changing his name."

"How old is he?"

"Forty-three."

"He was born a year after Dr. Wilson's death."

Chapter Forty-One

MOTHER & SON

Officer Graham

Detective Campbell wanted us to speak with Stanley first, but his mother insisted she speak to us. Alone.

"May I have some tea?" she asked sweetly.

"Officer Graham, would you mind?" Detective Campbell said.

"Yeah, sure," I said, standing up. I closed the meeting room door behind me and headed for the small kitchenette. I passed Stanley, who was sitting hunched over in a chair outside of the meeting room. He was chewing on his fingernails.

He glanced up and smiled, then did a double take when he realized it was me. "Are you done?" he asked nervously.

"No sir, we just started. Your mom wants tea."

"Oh, let me help you," he said, standing. "She likes it a certain way, or she becomes cranky."

Stanley made his mom's tea in silence. He ensured she had the right amount of sugar, the tea was the right color and added a slice of lemon that another officer had offered. He carried the cup all the way to the meeting room, but when I opened the door, I took the cup from him.

"But," he said, glancing nervously inside.

"I'll take it from here," I said, entering the room and closing the door behind me. "Here's your tea."

"What did I tell you, Detective. Stanley fusses over his mother. That boy can't do anything without me." She enjoyed a long sip. "Just the way I like it."

"Mrs. Whitaker," Detective Campbell said, "or should we call you Delilah Wilson."

Tea spilled all over the table. Detective Campbell and I lifted our notepads before everything got went.

"Oh deary, me, so sorry, boys. Please forgive me," she said, pulling out a tissue from her vintage clutch handbag. "I'm terribly clumsy sometimes."

"Was it something I said?" Detective Campbell said, cleaning his area with a napkin.

I had a handkerchief to clean my space, then placed my notebook back down.

"Yes, that's my name," she said, averting her eyes.

"What was Christopher's last day like?" Detective Campbell flicked his pen. "Was he upset, angry, scared?"

With a shaky hand, Mrs. Whitaker set her cup down, pulled out another clean tissue, and wiped the few drops on her hand. "I don't know. I came home and found him hanging in the garage. It was a terribly sad day."

"Why is that?"

"I'd found out I was pregnant, and my husband killed himself. And since that day, I've struggled every bit of the way. My life hasn't been easy, Detective."

"It couldn't have been that bad." Detective Campbell flicked his pen again, making her glance at his hand. "You live in a double story house that's paid off. You put Stanley through medical school, and you never worked a day in your life until Stanley gave you a job. Why is that? Were you bored, or did you want to keep an eye on him?"

"I don't know what you're trying to say, Detective. I love Stanley and want to help him."

"Do you think Christopher was guilty of hurting all those people?" Detective Campbell said, then clicked his pen.

Mrs. Whitaker flinched. "Yes, he made deadly mistakes, which he paid for with his life."

"Seems like an easy way out," Detective Campbell mumbled, and clicked his pen again. Mrs. Whitaker stared at his hand like she wanted to squash it. "Tell us how you killed Ella." I'd never heard him sound so insensitive before, but it made sense. He didn't want Mrs. Whitaker sensing hesitation in his questioning.

"I don't know what you mean. I had nothing to do with her death. Ella and my Stanley dated. She dated many men. Then one of them got rid of her. Stanley could never hurt anyone on purpose; he's a good boy. He isn't like Christopher."

"What about Daniel?"

"Who is Daniel?" she said, glancing away.

"He's one of Ella's boyfriends. Maybe Daniel found out that Stanley killed Ella and was blackmailing him. He wanted to divorce his wife and needed money. Stanley didn't like that someone else knew about what he did, and he staged Daniel's death to look like a suicide."

Mrs. Whitaker giggled. "You're reaching, Detective. My Stanley would never think of such things, never mind doing it. He's a—"

"Good boy, yes, you've said so. Maybe it was you,

Delilah?" Detective Campbell said. "Maybe it was you all along?" He clicked his pen.

"Detective," she said, raising her fragile hands, "I'm an old woman. How on earth could I do any of those things?"

"I don't know." Detective Campbell opened the case folder and placed the pictures of Ella in front of her. She didn't look away or complain about the graphic content. She just stared at the black-and-white pictures, as if she were admiring them.

"What happened that day?" Detective Campbell asked after a couple of minutes had passed, but she didn't answer.

She stared at the pictures, deep in thought.

"Did you and Ella have a fight?"

She continued staring in silence.

"Is Officer Aldridge Stanley's father?" he asked, changing the subject. He clicked his pen.

Mrs. Whitaker slowly glanced up at Detective Campbell. Her dark eyes twinkling with sinister humor, and the corners of her mouth tilted upward slightly.

"Did Aldridge help destroy evidence connecting you to Ella's death?"

She stared quietly, leaning back in the chair, and folded her arms across her chest.

"Did you cut her up or did your good boy do it considering he's the surgeon?" Detective Campbell leaned back in his chair, staring deadpan at her. "If you aren't going to say anything, perhaps we should chat with Stanley. Tell him we know what he's done, and that we have a nice cell waiting for him. Officer Graham, please take him to the meeting room next door."

"Yes, Detective," I said, standing.

"No!" Mrs. Whitaker slammed her hand on the table. "Leave Stanley out of this. He did nothing." She stared at me, her expression a warning. I wasn't sure what she could do to me. Eugene was no longer here to help her. And based on her reaction, she didn't want Stanley knowing the truth about what she did.

"The truth always comes out Delilah," Detective Campbell said. His tone was clinical, sending chills up my spine.

I stood frozen, unsure whether I should fetch Stanley or stay here and help Detective Campbell in case the old woman tried to lunge at him and scratch his eyes out.

"Please sit," she said to me.

I glanced at Detective Campbell, who nodded. I sat down.

She leaned forward and sighed. "Christopher was not a nice man. He used to beat me before he took his frustration out on his patients. It relieved me he'd found another way to get rid of it, but it saddened me how he'd hurt them. I was the one who gave the information to the police, to Officer Aldridge, and that Detective Payne. And when Christopher found out, he beat me so badly I stopped breathing for a few seconds. He brought me back to life and he never let me forget it."

Mrs. Whitaker had a long drink of her tea to catch her breath. "Officer Aldridge provided me with affection I'd never experienced before. Christopher never wanted children, saying if I ever fell pregnant, he'd cut the child out of me and throw it in the garbage disposal. While Eugene was gentle and treated me tenderly; I felt safe in his arms. Then when they brought the case against Christopher and charged him with all those crimes, he was going to run away, he was going to get away with it all. He emptied our joint bank accounts and packed his bag. I couldn't allow him to get away, Detective, so I drugged Christopher and called Eugene to help me."

She stood and walked to the corner. She seemed fragile as she stretched her legs. "After Christopher exhaled his last breath and was in the ground, Eugene wanted me to move in with him. I said no, obviously, it would look suspicious. Then, when I found out I was pregnant with his child, he asked me to marry him. I said no again, because Christopher stipulated in his will that should I remarry, I'd lose everything, and his money given to his awful sister. I couldn't allow that to happen. That was my money; I deserved every penny.

"I told Eugene to marry that wonderful woman. What was her name?" She snapped her fingers. "Oh, never mind. She was good for him. They couldn't fall pregnant, unfortunately, so I allowed Eugene to visit the boy, but only until he started asking questions. Then I forbid it. I didn't want to confuse Stanley about who his father was, even though Christopher was a bad man. And I didn't want anyone finding out how I knew Eugene. It was all a delicate balancing act. To smooth things over with Eugene, I gave Stanley Eugene's mother's maiden name while I kept my last name. I didn't want Stanley's reputation as a doctor tarnished before it even began. He married a lovely girl after he qualified as a doctor, but she died of cancer before he specialized as a surgeon. Then my Stanley threw himself into his job, until that Ella girl came along and changed him, and not in a good way. He started talking back to me, wanting to move me into a retirement home, and all that nonsense. I didn't like that; I'd given that boy everything. I'd never give up what was rightfully mine without a fight."

"Did you make him help you kill her?"

She shook her head. "No, he knew nothing about what I'd done."

"Eugene helped with everything?"

"Yes."

"Who cut her up?"

"I did," she said. Those two words were as cold as she was. "I knew enough about the body and what to use to ensure I could cut her in half with little effort."

"Why make it look like The Black Dahlia murder?" I asked. Amazed, I'd thought of the question before Detective Campbell.

"Christopher," she said. "He told me so much about that unsolved murder. I thought he did it himself. I didn't know him around the time she was killed, I thought that maybe," she shrugged, "it was him. He had mentioned it so many times I remembered it and thought, why not copy it. Send the police in a different direction."

"Then what?" Detective Campbell asked.

"Stanley asked many questions. Where was I? What had I been doing? I told him I was with a friend. Then when my poor son saw her body, he fell into a deep depression for a long time. He barely spoke to me, only worked a few days a week. These last five years passed quickly, and Stanley slowly worked his way out of his sadness. I started working for him to keep an eye on him. We were doing okay when you boys came around and started asking questions. It made Stanley anxious, and he followed you to find out what you knew. He wanted to find the killer more than anything."

Now I remembered where we'd seen Stanley. He wore the fedora hat at Charlie's. It all made sense now, and I imagined how those events could change someone. To lose them instantly and so brutally would send anyone into a depression, especially if they loved that person. And from the sounds of it, Stanley loved Ella.

"What about Daniel?" Detective Campbell asked.

I circled what Dr. Brink had said about his murder.

"Daniel saw us hanging around the motel that evening. But he didn't know we were there for Ella. After you spoke to him at his cabin, he phoned me, inviting me around. I went. He asked questions and I couldn't lie to him. But he knew too much and wanted to phone you. When he pulled out your card, I had to do something."

I glanced at this old lady, wondering how she did it.

"It wasn't difficult at all," she continued, smiling; like she knew people saw her as this fragile old woman when in fact she was the opposite. "I added a drug to his drink and led him upstairs. I held my gun on him to ensure he did as I asked. Then, after I tied his hands, he seemed to wake up. I realized I hadn't given him a large enough dose and kicked him off before he got the chance to hurt me."

"And you wore a pair of men's boots?" Detective Campbell said.

"I used Daniel's shoes to cause confusion."

"Did you wear your blue jersey?" I asked, remembering our first encounter with her.

"Yes, it's my favorite."

Chapter Forty-Two

CHARGED

Officer Graham

Officer Crick neared. "Just the officer I'm looking for," he said. "I've booked the old lady. Her lawyer is on his way, and her son won't leave."

"Thanks," I said, noticing his watch. "New?" I asked, pointing at it.

"Yeah," he said. "How did she do it? She said nothing while I processed her." He fidgeted with his watch. "How can that little old lady kill anyone? She seems so fragile."

"We're still busy with the report," I said, waving the statement she signed. "Let me find Stanley before he gets stuck somewhere he's not supposed to." I walked away.

"Can't you tell me something?" he said, grabbing my upper arm.

I stopped and stared down at Officer Crick's hand. "Do you mind?" I said, prying his fingers off me one at a time. The lines between my brows deepened. "Why are you so interested in this case?"

"You know," he said, raising a shoulder. His face had reddened. "I'm just interested in it. It's The Black Dahlia all over again." He nervously glanced away.

"Are you the one speaking to the newspaper?"

"What? Me, nah, man." He waved me away and hurried down the corridor.

Detective Campbell neared and shrugged. "What's that about?"

"I don't know. He seems too interested in the case."

"It's a big case. I don't blame him."

"Is anyone else asking as many questions as he is, though? We've just charged her."

"No, no one else has asked me anything. Do you think—"

"Yeah, I'm going to follow him," I said.

"Okay, you go do that and I'll find Stanley."

I hurried down the corridor but didn't see which room he'd entered. Voices sounded on my left, and I closed the gap.

"Yeah, yeah," Officer Crick said. "We've charged her with Ella's and Daniel's murder." Silence. "What? No, her son did nothing. Yeah. Yeah. Okay. I'll expect the same amount." Silence.

Two officers approached, speaking loudly.

"Listen, I got to go," Officer Crick said.

I leaned against the wall and waited.

Officer Crick exited and flinched when he saw me.

"You owe Captain Payne an explanation," I said, grabbing his arm.

"Then what happened?" Detective Campbell said, enjoying my story.

"Captain Payne suspended him without pay pending an investigation," I said, smiling. Then quickly schooled my features. I didn't want to feel that much joy when someone else suffered, but he deserved the punishment. If he'd said something to the reporter that could've jeopardized our case, we wouldn't be sitting here with the killer behind bars.

"Good," Detective Campbell said. "Stanley is in the meeting room. And I've called a psychologist to speak with him. He seems to have difficulty processing everything."

"Okay," I said, "I hope he gets the help he needs." It relieved me justice would be served, but I also felt bad for the guy. His mother murdered his girl and now he'd lost them both; it's terrible what he was going through and understood why he was struggling.

"Boys," Captain Payne barked as he rounded the corner. I flinched. "My office," he said and disappeared down the corridor.

"How does he do that?" Detective Campbell said, chuckling. "He's like the corridor ninja, popping out of nowhere to yell instructions."

"I hope that's a good sign," I said, feeling nervous.

We followed Captain Payne to his office and sat in his visitor chairs.

"Well done on closing this case," Captain Payne said, settling into his chair. "I'm sure Officer Graham has filled you in about Officer Crick," he asked Detective Campbell, but pointed at me.

"Yes, Captain."

"Good, now aside from that, you two work well together and I was wondering if you'd like to make it a permanent thing?"

Detective Campbell nodded. "Yeah, sure," he said, smiling at me.

"Thank you, Captain," I said, feeling relieved. I enjoyed working with Detective Campbell and had a lot still to learn from him.

"I understand you were looking into the evidence tampering of that Jack case," Captain Payne said, staring at me. My clothing clung to my body. "And that we may have found the culprit." He leaned forward with his elbows on his desk and steepled his fingers. "I'm bitterly disappointed, Officer Graham, but I understand. You were going through a slice of your own hell at the time. I should report you to Internal Affairs," he paused for effect. No doubt wanting me to sweat a little more. "But I know you won't make the same mistake twice. I believe in giving people a second chance. Don't make me regret it." He arched a bushy eyebrow for effect.

Detective Campbell shifted uncomfortably beside me. I wanted to glare at him for telling Captain, but my focus remained on the man speaking.

"And before you accuse your partner, he told me nothing about the video. I've been doing my own investigation and figured it out; it's that weird gait of yours, Officer. I'm amazed Officer Crick didn't see it first, but I suspect he wanted money from you."

I nodded, even though he didn't ask me a question.

"Right, I'm suspending you for two days, no pay, and you," he pointed at Detective Campbell, "can take your lovely wife away for her birthday weekend. I'll see you both early on Tuesday. Now go before I change my mind." He waved us away.

I closed the door behind me.

"I said nothing, I swear," Detective Campbell said, raising both hands.

"It's okay," I said, wiping the nervous sweat from my forehead. "I deserved worse, but I'll happily take these two days off; I need it."

Chapter Forty-Three

THE ICE FOREST

Ella

I walked with Kevin to his vehicle and watched him climb inside. As he reversed out of the parking, I waved.

"Hey darling," a man said behind me.

I flinched and spun around. My heart racing in my chest. "What are you doing here?" The lines between my brows deepened. I glanced around.

"I'm looking for you," Daniel said, smiling. "I was going to surprise you early tomorrow morning, but I was across the street buying milk when I saw you with Kevin."

I smiled, rocked onto my toes, and kissed him. "That's okay. Where are you off to now?"

"Home. I had a long day at The Lounge, so I'm looking forward to doing nothing."

"I don't suppose you want to have a drink with me before you go?" I asked, not wanting to be alone now.

"I'd love to," he said, opening the door for me.

I entered the restaurant again, and the same server

greeted us. She did a double take, smiled at me, and escorted us to a table.

"See me tomorrow," he blurted as I sat down.

"Daniel, we've already seen each other this week."

"I know, but I want to take you to a pottery lesson. It's something you've always wanted to do, isn't it? And I need to spend time with you." He reached for my hands. "Please?" he asked with pleading eyes. "I miss you."

"Fine," I said, unable to say no to pottery lessons. I've always wanted to try.

"It's going to be fun, you'll see."

I closed the door to the motel room and kicked off my shoes. It was only nine, but I was ready to sleep. The evening had been busy and emotional. The men in my life were becoming more demanding of my time, and I didn't know what to do. I didn't want to 'throw' any of them away, and I couldn't choose between them. They each had something I loved, but also something I didn't like, which deterred me from committing to any of them.

Boundaries. I had no boundaries with any of them. I was a people pleaser, said 'yes' to things even though I didn't want to do it, and because of this I suffered in the end. It tired me out, and like now, I desperately needed to recharge my batteries.

A nice hot bath would do me good. I could add some candles, sip on some wine, and enjoy the quiet evening.

I reached for my bag and pulled out my nightgown when a knock sounded on the door. I groaned and approached the door.

"Who is it?" I called, not wanting to open it. Nobody knew I was here.

"Ella, it's Officer Aldridge."

"Has something happened to Stanley?" I asked as anxiety flooded my system. I knew he was a family friend of theirs.

"Yes, you need to come with me."

"How did you know I was here?" I asked, cautiously opening the door.

"You must come with me," he said, frowning. The lines between his dark brown eyes deepened, and he pursed his lips. There was something in his expression that reminded me of Stanley that day his mother angered him.

"How did you know I was here?" I asked again, closing the door slightly.

"I've been looking everywhere for you, Ella," he said, sounding strange. "Stanley is in trouble, and I've been driving around. It was by chance I passed here and noticed you entering this room."

"Oh," I said, hesitating. The Roadside Inn was out of anyone's way unless they came here specifically. It's possible Stanley's mother had told Officer Aldridge that I came here sometimes. "Let me grab my jacket."

I was tired and wanted desperately to sleep, but if something had happened to Stanley, then I needed to be with him. A cold wind slammed into the door, opening it wider. There was a light shining behind Officer Aldridge, outlining his body in darkness.

I pulled on my black turtleneck jersey, then my warm jacket, and followed him to his car.

"The forest?" I said, feeling unsure about agreeing to this. "What's Stanley doing out here this time of the evening."

"There was an accident."

Snow continued falling, covering the ground in a thick blanket of ice. The once green trees were now completely white.

"What kind of accident?" I asked, as worry enveloped me.

Officer Aldridge parked the car, climbed out, and opened my side. He pulled something out of the back seat and covered my shoulders. "In case you're cold," he said, smiling. "I don't know what he was doing here, but his mother asked that I fetch you before the police arrive."

"Is he dead?" I asked, and dread filled my veins. It devastated me to hear that something bad had happened to Stanley. I couldn't believe what was happening. I had just spoken with him and now this. In a blink of an eye, my life had changed, and Stanley was gone forever.

Officer Aldridge led me up the path toward an area I knew some used to picnic or continue on the hiking trail. We walked off the trail between trees, curved left and right, which left me confused.

"Where are you going?" I asked, shivering even though I had the blanket around my shoulders. "Officer Aldridge," I said, cringing because I hated whining, but I needed to understand what was going on and where Stanley was.

"Here," he said, standing back. It was a spot I'd never seen before. Trees surrounded an area in an almost perfect circle and in the center was a large black bag, a table and chair, a lantern, and a gas stove with a kettle. The kettle whistled. "Tea?" He offered.

"What's going on? Where is Stanley?" I nervously glanced around.

He ignored my question and dusted the snow off the chair. "Sit," he demanded.

A coldness not related to the weather settled in my bones. I did as instructed and sat on the chair. I glanced up, the bright silver moon pulling my attention. When footsteps crunched ice behind me, I flinched.

"Have a sip." The female voice said behind me.

I craned my neck to see Stanley's mother glowering down at me. The beautiful silver moon spoiled by her angry features.

"Drink deary," she said in her sweet, yet aggressive tone.

I had a small sip. The sharp, bitter taste taking my breath away, making me choke. I spat out the liquid in the snow beside me; it was brown. "What is this?" I asked, shuddering. "And where is Stanley?"

"He's not here to help you," Mother Awful said, closing the gap. "That's not enough," she yelled. "Have a bigger sip." She pointed her finger at the cup. Officer Aldridge neared, taking the cup from my hands, and stuck his thumb in my mouth and pulled my jaw open.

"No," I cried, grabbing his arm and pulling him away. His thumb was almost out when something grabbed me from behind; cold, hard fingers gripping my arms, and I loosened my grip on him. "No…"

Officer Aldridge pushed my head against Mrs. Whitaker's front. Her bony hands gripping me tighter. Officer Aldridge opened my mouth wider and poured more of the warm, bitter liquid down my throat. I coughed and spluttered. Half the liquid flowed out of my mouth, down my chin and onto the blanket around my shoulders. Unfortunately, I swallowed some of the stuff and it burned down my throat and stomach.

Almost immediately, a warm sensation coursed through my veins, numbing my muscles.

"There, there, deary," Mother Awful said. "I want things to go my way, and you're not included." Mrs. Whitaker came into view. Her devilish grin splitting her evil face in two.

"Why? I love your son," I mumbled, but the words were unintelligible.

She patted the top of my head. "Exactly, deary, exactly."

"This is wrong," Officer Aldridge said. "I don't want to do this."

"Do this or our son is going to ruin his life. Do you want that to happen?" she yelled.

"No, but this is wrong, Delilah. We're hurting another human."

"That's not what you said about Chris. You were all too happy getting rid of him."

"That was different. He was hurting his patients."

"She's hurting my patience, and my son by sleeping with all those men. She's a whore Eugene. A whore. Do you want our son paying the price? Because that's what's going to happen if you don't do as I say."

My fingers moved involuntarily. The heat in my veins subsided, and the burning in my tummy calmed. My toes moved. I needed to get away from these two.

"Delilah."

"Eugene, help me."

Officer Aldridge visibly sighed. He didn't want to do this, but she was holding something against him, forcing him to do this by manipulating him.

He scowled at her, but she wasn't looking.

She cackled like a witch. "Hurry," she said, removing

items from the table and packing them in the bag. "We don't want anyone finding us here."

Mrs. Whitaker, Mother Awful, and Officer Aldridge cleaned the area, leaving no trace behind.

Feeling returned to my muscles. My skin tingled with pins and needles, my hands moved, my legs moved.

"We can leave this one's body over there," she said, pointing at a ditch.

No, I couldn't allow them to kill me and dump my body here like trash. I had to do everything I could to get away from them.

Lights up ahead blinded me.

"What's that?" Officer Aldridge asked, turning around.

Before he could fold the table, I kicked it, sending it flying into his face. I stood, backhanded Mrs. Whitaker, and she fell backward into the snow. I tightened my grip on the blanket and ran toward the lights. The lights disappeared. Panic settled. I ran left, then right in search of those lights or footprints, but the snow had already covered it.

I ran and ran and ran. It felt like I'd been running for hours and was nowhere near the exit. I was running so fast, a tree root gripped my foot, sending me tumbling forward. A boulder stopped me from crashing into the icy stream below. I climbed onto the boulder, my black shirt hooking onto a tree branch. I yanked it free, tearing at my top. The blanket fell off my shoulders. Something dripped down my face and into my mouth; my nose was bleeding.

"Hello?" I said, seeing four flashlights in the distance. "Help," I called. I jumped off the boulder and headed in their direction when something hard crashed into my side, sending us into the ground.

People called out to me. They whistled. They wanted to help.

I'm here, I said, but no words left my mouth.

I couldn't move. My head ached. The weight lifted off my side. I sucked in air. A wetness dripped onto my cheek.

"I'm so sorry," he said. "I don't want to do this. Forgive me."

"What are you doing?" That awful woman said. "Hurry, carry her to the car. We need to go before they see us. I have a better plan."

Chapter Forty-Four

FRIENDS IN STRANGE PLACES

Stanley

Detective Campbell called the lawyer Mother had asked for. He sat beside me, going over the various charges against her. I still couldn't believe it. Mother. Officer Aldridge; my real father. They murdered Christopher. Murdered Ella. I didn't know in which direction to go in; hate Mother for hurting Ella or celebrating her for how they stopped Christopher from hurting his patients.

"I've called a psychologist to come see you," Detective Campbell said, paging through a document.

"For me or Mother?"

"For you," he said, closing the document.

"I'm fine, thanks." I folded my arms across my chest.

"Just in case." Detective Campbell leaned back in the chair. "Can I get you some coffee or something to eat?"

"I'm fine, thanks," I said, rubbing my face, and pushed my chair back. My chest ached. Leaning on my elbows on my knees, I rested my head in my hands. "I can't believe it, you know. It was Mother all this time." I sat up, blinking back tears.

"Yeah, she wanted to control every aspect of your life, even the women you dated."

I shook my head. "But to kill. That's extreme. Ella hurt nobody."

"She desperately wanted Ella out of your life."

Although I understood what Mother had done, I still couldn't fathom the idea that my mom, the woman who gave birth to me, had done this. She had sliced Ella in two and destroyed her beautiful smile. Mother tortured and mutilated my girlfriend.

I should've seen this coming. Mother had already tried to hurt Ella once, but I didn't think she would try again. I would forever live with the consequences of my actions, and the guilt for not protecting Ella like I'd promised.

My hands bunched into fists as heat spread throughout my body; anger replacing sadness. "I want her gone forever," I said, surprised by the emotionless tone of my voice. "I want Mother to rot in jail."

"You don't need help getting your wish," Detective Campbell said. "By processing her fingerprints, we got a match from the prints we found on Ella's body. She also confessed to all three murders."

"Good." All the hairs on my body stood on end. It relieved me Mother would never set foot in my house ever again, and she would never try to control my life. She wouldn't be anywhere near me. "I need to get out of here."

"You don't want to wait for the lawyer?" he asked, standing.

"Nah, I've got better things to do with my time." I stood and headed for the exit.

"She felt nothing," Detective Campbell said, following me out.

"What do you mean?"

"Ella, she was already dead when your mother started mutilating her body. Ella wouldn't have felt anything."

"Thanks, Detective. It brings some comfort, but not much. Mother took her away from us too soon. I'll never forgive her for what she's done." I continued walking, heading for the exit, leaving the detective behind me.

I felt the warmth of the sun on my face. It was late afternoon with a slight breeze. I traversed down the stairs and headed for my vehicle, wanting desperately to get away and go on a drive that lasted weeks; anything to forget what Mother had done.

Chapter Forty-Five

WEEKEND AWAY

Detective Steve Campbell

Alice's head fell gently to the side, her eyes closed, and her mouth slightly ajar. The warm sun splashed across her body, ensuring she kept warm while I drove.

We followed the quiet winding road toward our cabin and all I could think about was this case we just closed. I should be thinking about Alice and our weekend away, but I thought about Delilah, Christopher, Eugene, Stanley, and all the men in Ella's life. But most of all, I thought of Ella. That poor girl had gone through so much, she gave up so much of herself, and the rest just took, took, took.

Alice stirred; her eyelids flitted open. "Are we there yet?" she asked lazily and stretched out her legs.

"Almost," I said, reaching for her hand and kissing the top. "I hope you're ready to do nothing but eat, go for walks, and nap."

"Haha, absolutely," she said, sitting upright.

I put the indicator on and turned left onto the dirt road;

the woods becoming thicker and greener. I opened the window, the cool air smelling of pine, wet wood, and soil; it was beautiful. It relieved me there were no hints of copper or the sounds of sirens.

We arrived at our cabin, and I parked the car. Alice climbed out, almost running to the place.

"Oh, Steve, it's marvelous," she called out, closing her eyes and spun in a circle.

I stood beside her as we surveyed our home away from home for the next couple of days. "Beautiful, isn't it?" I said, snaking my arms around her waist.

"It's going to be lovely here." Her smile reached her eyes.

"I'll get our bags," I said, leaving her on the deck with the splash pool.

Once our luggage was in our room, I made a fire in the living room, while Alice made us tea. We sat on the deck admiring the view, drinking tea and eating cookies.

"I'm thinking of making us sandwiches for lunch."

"Sounds good," I said. "I'll get the hot tub ready," I wiggled my eyebrows, "so we can enjoy our view and get a water massage."

"Haha, just what the doctor ordered."

Chapter Forty-Six

BACK TO WORK

Detective Steve Campbell

The Roadside Inn clerk opened room number nine and headed toward the middle of the room. "Like I was telling the officer, I was cleaning here," he pointed at the bed, "I moved it to the side because we haven't cleaned here in like forever, and I discovered this." He pushed the bed to one side. The air vent was open and, on the carpet, laid torn out pages from a notebook and polaroids.

James neared and snapped photographs. He picked up the polaroids and whistled. "It's our girl," he said, handing them to me. I flipped through the pictures of Ella with gloved hands. They were of the wounds inflicted on her by Diane. I handed them to Officer Graham, who bagged them. "Her diary entry," James added, handing them to me one page at a time.

The diary entry detailed Diane's sexual assault on Ella. "This will help our case against Diane," I said, handing them to Officer Graham. "And Kevin rented this room that evening?"

"Yes, sir, the fourteenth of January nineteen-ninety-seven," the clerk said, nodding and handing me a copy of the bookings schedule. I gave it to Officer Graham.

"Thanks," I said, not remembering the clerk's name. "Was there any luggage left here that night?"

"No, sir," the clerk said. "I would've remembered if there was anything, but no, they left the key on the counter sometime during that night, and they'd paid up before checking in. So, I thought nothing strange."

"Thanks for calling us about the items."

"Pleasure, sir," the clerk said, heading for the door. "Call me if you need anything, but I have people that need checking in."

"Three people phoned me about Diane," I said, walking around the small room.

"Is she out on bail?" Officer Graham asked.

"No, the judge denied her bail. She's never getting out again," I said. It brought a sense of accomplishment knowing Diane, a female predator, won't hurt anyone else again. She might try to while in jail, but that was different. She'd never hurt an innocent woman ever again.

"And Jessica?" Officer Graham said, handing the evidence to James. "Have you heard what's happening to her?"

"Not yet, but I suspect she'll go away for a while, too. Her lawyer told me she had to sell her apartment to pay for his fees." I felt a twinge of satisfaction. The women who had done Ella harm would go away for a long time.

"Great job," James said, packing up his things. "I've got to rush off. There's a burglary that needs tending to."

"You have a good weekend off?" I asked once we were in the car and driving out of the parking area of the Inn.

"Yeah, I told Macey everything. She threatened to leave me, but once she calmed down, she understood. She begged me not to do anything stupid again."

"And?"

"What?"

"Will you do something stupid again?" I grinned.

"No, Detective. My stupid days are over. I'm on the straight and narrow." He chuckled.

"Good, because I enjoy working with you. Maybe we can see about you moving up in the ranks."

"Really?" he said, his tone filled with excitement.

"Yeah, really. I think it's time."

Officer Graham had paid his dues. It was senseless continuing the punishment. He had lost enough, had regrets. Now he needed to move forward and live a little.

"Besides," I said, smiling, "we've got criminals to catch, and it would be a waste not having you work with me."

"Thank you, Detective. I genuinely appreciate it." He visibly relaxed. "It's going to be a good day."

We merged with traffic when a shot rang out. Our windscreen shattered. Something warm struck my face. Officer Graham winced. He fell onto my shoulder. I slammed on brakes, taking cover. With my weapon trained in the direction the shot had come from, but they had already gone in the opposite direction.

"Officer Graham?" I panicked when I tried moving him off me. I reached for the radio to call it in. "Officer down, I repeat, officer down."

The Dana Mulder Suspense Thriller Series

vinci-books.com/deadlypattern

Natalie Michaels writing as N Gray

When a standard medical procedure ends with a girl missing and another dead, the case lands on Dana's desk.

Dana's search uncovers a chilling pattern: a respected doctor with a deadly obsession for his patients. But with only circumstantial evidence, taking him down seems impossible.

Turn the page for a free preview…

Deadly Pattern: Chapter One

Bianca stretched her legs. That familiar click in her right knee sent a jolt of pain up her leg; the movement caused her to move her upper body, and pain from her shoulder made her wince. She relaxed one muscle at a time, and, after a few seconds, the pain dissipated. Having another scar once she'd healed wasn't comforting, but it was just another scar to add to the one that went down her right leg.

When Bianca had first arrived at the hospital, she had shared a room with another patient before being wheeled into surgery. Now she had a private room and wondered whether her insurance had approved it in full, because she didn't have money to pay the difference should there be an outstanding balance.

Her room was clean with the standard eggshell-colored walls, starched bedding, and repulsive hospital smell—disinfectant mixed with body odor and the lingering stench of a corpse or two.

Her shoulder throbbed, and the joint felt tight. She tried to move it, but it was strapped tightly in a sling against her body. It was an old sports injury that had worsened when she had fallen. She couldn't remember how she had fallen on the sidewalk; she was walking one second, the next thing she had woken in the back of someone's truck. The kind man had offered to take her to the hospital. The next day, she was scheduled for a rotator cuff repair.

Gently massaging against the bandage on her shoulder, she felt something, and wondered whether the orthopedic surgeon had done an arthroscopy as he had promised or if he had gone full on butcher on her arm. She shuddered at the thought.

Footsteps sounded; a light knock on the door was followed by a nurse beaming at Bianca as she entered. "Morning, my name is Mary, and I'll tend to you today. How ya feeling?" The nurse wore a tight white bun on top of her head, had clear crystal-blue eyes, and a warm smile to match her happy demeanor. She carried a blood pressure monitor and reached for Bianca's arm. Her powdery perfume wafted in behind her, causing Bianca to stifle a sneeze.

"Okay, I guess. When will I see the doctor?" Bianca sat up, using her uninjured arm. Her right arm throbbed in the sling as she moved even though she kept it still. She leaned against the pillow, breathless. She could stay where she was. She didn't have the strength to sit all the way upright; that position was as good as it would get.

"He's busy with other patients, but you'll see him soon," Mary said while leaning Bianca forward, fluffed her pillows then helped her lay back again. "You comfy now?"

Bianca nodded. "And my dad, is he here yet?"

"No, but I'll send him in the moment he gets here." Mary squeezed her knee through the starched bedding.

"Don't fret. I'm sure he'll visit you soon." She cocked her head with a sympathetic smile. "You hungry?"

"Not really. Maybe thirsty." Bianca felt blood drain from her face. The sudden movements didn't agree with her, and bile rose, which she swallowed, tasting the bitter aftereffects of the anesthesia.

Mary smiled knowingly. "It's just the morphine. It makes patients a little nauseated soon after the procedure. Don't panic with what I'm about to do." Mary lifted the bleached covers. "I'm just going to remove the catheter."

Bianca felt a gentle tug on her lower body but didn't notice the little tube leaving her. She did have an overwhelming need to urinate though.

Mary unhooked the bag from the side of her bed and placed it on the trolley that stood against the far wall.

Bianca relaxed, hoping the feeling would disappear, but it didn't, and she needed to go. "Okay, I need the bathroom now." Bianca slowly sat upright.

Mary smiled, pulled the covers all the way back and helped her off the bed.

Bianca wobbled slightly, but Mary steadied and guided her to the small bathroom in the corner.

Once Bianca was done and back in bed, Mary left the room but returned after a few seconds, wheeling a trolley full of food and a glass of juice to Bianca's bedside. She set the plate of food onto the over-bed table with cutlery and a plastic cup with three capsules. "Eat." She sat in the chair beside the bed and watched intently.

"Are you going to watch me eat the whole time?" Bianca lifted the lid to see scrambled eggs and toast.

"They say eggs and dry toast go down easier on the first day. Don't mind me. I'm here to ensure you're okay and can eat something before you take your pain meds." She jerked her chin at the plastic cup holding the capsules.

Bianca ate slowly and sipped even slower on the orange juice then paused until the nausea passed before she continued eating.

Mary watched Bianca the entire time. Frosted-colored eyes gleamed at her once she finished. "Now for your medicine, it'll help with the pain. I promise." Mary pushed the plastic cup closer along with the half-full glass of orange juice.

Bianca swallowed one capsule at a time, finishing the orange juice.

Mary removed the plate and glass and handed her the remote for the television against the wall opposite her bed.

She flicked through the channels—all six of them—eventually stopping on a cartoon about a mouse. Bianca's eyelids felt heavy. Her skin tingled, and her body relaxed one muscle at a time. The medication took its hold on her.

When Mary closed the door behind her, Bianca's eyes fluttered open, alarmed when she heard the door shut with a distinct sound of a lock turning.

Bianca's heart hammered against her chest. Why was she locked in?

Deadly Pattern: Chapter Two

I watched the black whirlpool in my favorite mug as I stirred my coffee. The warm liquid tasted like coffee for once and not burnt tar. That's only because I was the first one at the office and had started the pot. I was usually the last to arrive, but I was up early this morning.

"Where did these come from?" I asked Marc, pointing at the bouquet on my desk.

"Dunno. They were outside the door when I arrived. The card had your name on it, so I placed it on your desk while you were in the kitchen making coffee. Do you have a boyfriend we don't know about?"

"No! No time for that." I surveyed the card. It only contained my name printed—not even the company who had delivered the flowers. I shrugged. "They're pretty. It's a shame I have to throw them away."

Marc arched an eyebrow.

"Don't give me that look." I chuckled.

Marc arched the other eyebrow; it was his party trick.

"I don't trust flowers from unknown senders." I walked

toward the kitchen with the bouquet and placed them near the trashcan for discarding.

When I reentered the office, Marc was tapping a wooden stirrer on his desk while yapping away on the phone to some poor schmuck who probably said something he shouldn't have. I grinned when red blotches climbed his neck and spread to his cheeks. Yep, someone was pissing him off.

Marc was my boss. He had opened his private investigative business about five years ago. Our workload consisted mostly of couples who suspected their partner of cheating and wanted proof for the lawyers. We also investigated cold cases of missing people, theft, and surveillance. Every now and then, we worked with the police on active cases—but not often.

Before Marc was a PI, he had been a detective, and before that a marine. He still stayed in shape but lately had developed a soft belly and only shaved once a week. I'd met him when I was hospitalized; his wife Rachael was my roommate. She had been in a car accident, and he had lived in the ward with her while she had been in a coma. He had told me about his business, and I had told him about me, and he had offered me this job. Unfortunately, his wife, who was also his receptionist, didn't survive. They had discharged me the same day as her passing. I had attended her funeral a day later to offer my support. And since Rachael's death, Marc hadn't hired another receptionist. Her desk stayed empty but clean, and we all answered our own desk phones. And, as they say, the rest was history.

The doorbell chimed, the door slammed shut, then an old-ish white male entered, knocking over one of the visitor chairs. He made a beeline for me and didn't stop until he was at my desk.

I rose from my seat, hand extended.

His hands were sun-kissed with age spots.

"I'm Dana. Can I help you?"

The man shook my hand, nodding profusely, and swallowed hard. It sounded like it hurt. His eyes were red-rimmed, forehead beading with sweat, and his clothing clung to him like a second skin.

I glanced outside to see the clouds in front of the sun and the wind blowing; it wasn't that hot. Whatever was happening with this man was serious.

"Do you have any water?" the man asked, his tongue sticking to the inside of his mouth, and he swallowed again. "Sorry. Where's my manners? I'm Ned."

"Yeah, sure." I grabbed a polystyrene cup from the holder, filled it with chilled filtered water and handed it to him. "Please, sit." I motioned for the visitor chair near my desk.

He gulped the water with a satisfactory *aah* sound.

I filled it again and handed him the full cup. "You don't have an appointment." I was expecting a phone call any moment, so whatever the guy wanted, he had to be quick.

"No." He swallowed, blinking misty eyes. "No appointment, but you come highly recommended—the best in Illinois actually."

Smart move, we loved flattery.

"What's the matter, Ned? You seem"—I waved my hands in his general direction— "disturbed by something."

He emptied the cup, placed it on my desk and wiped his eyes with the palms of his hands.

Marc ended his call, and I knew he was listening without having to look in his direction.

"My daughter is missing."

I raised an eyebrow. "Have you tried the cops, Ned?"

They were the first line of contact in missing children cases. They had the resources to find kids quicker. We didn't, unless they were cold cases, and there was no rush to solve those.

"You don't understand. I dropped her off at the hospital yesterday morning for a procedure on her shoulder. But, when I returned to fetch her, she wasn't there. When I spoke to the administrator at admissions, she said my daughter was never there."

"I understand how stressed you must be. But again, I must ask, did you go to the cops? They're better equipped to handle missing children cases. We don't get involved in active cases."

"She's an adult." His voice was clipped, concise. "And yes, I was there. Filled in that damn form and was told to come back in a couple of days. By then, she could be dead. And besides, they're all busy with that accident on the highway anyway."

Oh yes, I had been watching the highlights this morning when carnage on the highway flashed in red on my TV screen—forty-eight cars, two trucks, and a school bus. They needed all available resources.

"But they have detectives who work missing cases," I confirmed again.

Ned sighed, glanced at Marc then back at me. "She didn't run away from home, and she doesn't have a boyfriend. She really isn't that kind of kid. Yesterday, the detectives said they'll see what they can do and contact me. When they didn't, I phoned today, and they said the hospital staff didn't even have her on record. They also spoke with the doctor, and he denied ever consulting with her. It's like she disappeared, and nobody saw anything. I'm back to square one. The police think she has a boyfriend I wasn't aware of and left town with him." Ned leaned back in the visitor's chair, looking deflated and miserable. "We're close. Especially after her mother died. She wouldn't leave me like that without saying where she was going."

I glanced in Marc's direction, arching an eyebrow. This was the usual spiel we got from parents with so-called missing children. How many moms and dads really knew their kids and what they were up to?

Marc shrugged and nodded. Fine. We would hear Ned out and see how we could help. I would also see which detectives were working his daughter's case.

"Okay, Ned, give me all the details." I switched on my phone and tapped the voice recording app in the top right corner without having to look. "You don't mind if I record you?"

He nodded.

"Great. I want to know everything, from the moment you woke up yesterday until you walked through our door." I grabbed the nearest pen and pulled my notepad closer. "Sorry if I sound unsympathetic, but can you afford our rates?" I gestured toward the sign on the wall near my desk.

Ned checked the posted per-hour cost and nodded with widened eyes. "I own a construction company. It's fine."

We were not cheap, but we got results, and we got them quickly.

"I can take this case, Dana," Marc offered.

"It's fine, Marc. I got it."

"You have enough on your plate."

We'd had this conversation before, and I wasn't about to get into it with him again, especially not in front of a client.

"I. Got. It. Marc."

My desk phone rang. It was my other client. I glanced at Marc and asked with my eyes.

"Let me get that for you," Marc offered, punched numbers on his phone and answered my call.

I returned my attention to Ned.

He reviewed every single detail he could remember. He gave me all the names of the doctors his daughter had seen, along with the reasons, and when.

Deadly Pattern: Chapter Three

Bianca woke feeling groggy and nauseated . The last thing she remembered after eating the eggs was drinking the capsules. Then she slept.

Lifting the covers, she realized she was wearing different clothing. Someone had changed her underwear and nightie while she had slept. She lifted her arm to her nose and noticed her skin smelled of coconut. While she slept, they had cleaned her and covered her in the body cream. They had touched her. She whimpered and pulled the covers tighter around her body.

Unsure of the time or day, since she didn't have her cell, she was unsure how long she had been asleep for. The room had no windows or clocks, and the television had no time. She was hungry, therefore must've slept at least eight hours.

Bianca's shoulder ached. She hadn't recognized any of the capsules and vowed to never drink them again, even if the pain in her shoulder killed her. She knew and understood shoulder pain, but the unknown was scarier.

The door lock sounded, and Mary entered, wheeling a

trolley. Bianca sat and leered at her. Her shoulder throbbed with a constant pain no matter how she rested her injured arm.

Mary parked the trolley, lifted a plate and stood in front of Bianca; her smile reached her eyes, crow's feet prominent. She proffered the plate of food.

"Hello, sleepyhead. For dinner, you have rump steak, roast vegetables, fries, and a cheese sauce on the side."

"How long was I asleep?"

"A while."

"Did you change my clothing?" Bianca twisted the covers against her chest.

"Yes, but don't worry, I didn't look." Mary winked.

Bianca shuddered at the thought of lying unconscious while Mary touched her.

Mary removed the silver cloche, assaulting Bianca's nose with heavenly aromas, and her stomach rumbled. Mary pulled the over-bed table closer and placed the food on top and neatly lay the cutlery beside the plate. Next to the plate was a tiny plastic cup with the familiar three tablets.

Bianca eyed them suspiciously then glanced up at Mary. "Has my dad come yet?"

"No, dear, not yet. Are you sure you told him you were at this hospital?"

"He dropped me off." Her voice raised, sounding angry, but she didn't care. "And where is my phone? I need to call my dad."

"I'll look for your belongings. But I think they misplaced them during your operation."

"How convenient!" Bianca crossed her arms, not believing a word. "When will I see the doctor? Surely, I don't have to stay here for more than one day for such a minor procedure!" Heat crept up her face with unchecked anger, and her body felt hot.

Mary leered at her. "Do as you're told, Bianca. I said he will come when he's ready."

Bianca flinched as if she were hit.

They stared at one another for a heartbeat, then Mary's icy-blue eyes defrosted. Her demonic smile returned to that friendly yet dangerous crescent shape and placed her hands on her hips. "Eat up," she said sweetly. "And I'll see what I can do about the doctor coming by. Okay?" Mary was as chipper as ever. The sound of her voice was grating.

Bianca bit her bottom lip to stop venomous words from flying out of her mouth. She was thinking of a couple of swear words or where Mary could put her food but decided against it. She didn't know Mary or what she was capable of doing and had gone to great lengths to abduct her. Bianca was also in pain and couldn't defend herself.

Mary skipped out of the room. Once again, the familiar click as Mary locked the door.

Bianca eyed the tablets. She ate the food, one delicious bite at a time, and felt guilty for enjoying it, knowing full well something was off with nurse Mary. She realized she couldn't confront Mary due to her fluctuating mood whenever she didn't approve of Bianca's behavior. Until she knew more about her situation and why she was here, she wouldn't anger Mary. But she wouldn't drink the tablets again.

After she ate, she grabbed the plastic cup holding the tablets and climbed off the bed. Standing over the toilet bowl, she poured the three capsules inside and flushed, watching them swirl around and disappear.

Bianca pressed her ear against the door; all she heard was the thrumming hum of the air conditioner. And then she heard … footsteps. Her heart sank to her feet, and she bolted for her bed. With the sudden movement, she pulled her right arm skew, which sent bolts of lightning up her neck and pain down her arm. The door clicked open. Bianca lay still, her eyes shut tight. Footsteps heavier than Mary's edged in, coming closer. Gripping the pillow with one hand, the other the mattress, Bianca knew how to lay still—to play dead. It was fight, flight, or just lay there and pretend you're asleep. Someone brushed her hair out of her face. Beads of sweat peppered her forehead. Surely, they would know she was only pretending.

"What did you give her?" The whispering voice was a baritone.

"The usual three," Mary replied full of confidence.

"Did you see her swallow them?" His voice held a warning Bianca recognized and trembled.

A hand slapping flesh echoed in the room, followed by a soft whimper. They scuffled, then their footsteps were quick as they exited, followed by the door slamming and locking shut with sounds of crying in the hallway.

Bianca sat upright, shivering in disgust. That was too close. She pulled her knees to her chest and hugged her legs, rocking herself to sleep.

Grab your copy…
vinci-books.com/deadlypattern

About the Author

Multi-genre author writing twisted endings...

N Gray is a USA Today Bestselling Author who lives in Cape Town, South Africa, with her daughter and adopted cat named Miss Beans.

During the day, she's an analyst and provider profiler for a medical insurance company. At night, she types on her curved keyboard, creating fictional characters some may love and others you want to kill yourself.

She writes in four genres: urban fantasy, thriller, horror, and paranormal romance.

She now writes under Natalie Michaels for her new thrillers and SD Syns for her new horrors.

Acknowledgments

Thank you to my readers, old and new, for taking a chance on my books.

You are the reason I write the stories I do. As long as you keep reading, I'll keep writing.

I'm truly humbled by your support and encouragement.

I hope you enjoyed reading The White Dahlia

I wish I could say I enjoyed writing it, because I kind of did, but I was also terribly sad.

This book was literally written through my tears…

It was *10 July 2024*. I was halfway writing The White Dahlia when my boyfriend of two years passed away suddenly from a heart attack. It devastated me. I could do nothing for two weeks except mend my shattered heart.

I turned to writing as my therapy. I wrote chapter after chapter, because I knew he'd want me to finish this book. He would want me to move forward.

Grief strikes us out of nowhere, smacking us in the face, and we're left to our own devices to find a way out of the darkness.

If you are ever in a room by yourself with nothing but tissues and tears, I hope you find the courage to claw yourself out of your despair. Write. Speak to a friend. Go for therapy. There's no shame in doing any of that.

I wish you well.

Now… about The White Dahlia…

I've always been fascinated with The Black Dahlia case and wanted to write about her. And book #3 in my Steve Campbell series was as good a time as any to write that story.

www.ingramcontent.com/pod-product-compliance
Lightning Source LLC
Chambersburg PA
CBHW011746010726
47498CB00012B/2955